The
Symbolism
of
COLOR

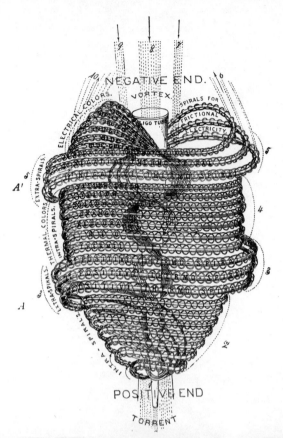

Edwin D. Babbitt's unique book on color in healing was published in 1878. The opening of the Brooklyn Bridge was celebrated in 1883, five years later. Babbitt amazingly wrote, "If such an atom should be set in the midst of New York City, it must create such a whirlwind that all its palatial structures, ships, bridges and surrounding cities, with two millions of people would be swept into fragments and carried into the sky." See Chapter X.

The
Symbolism
of
COLOR

By Faber Birren

A Citadel Press Book
Published by Carol Publishing Group

First Carol Publishing Group Edition 1989

Copyright © 1988 by Faber Birren

A Citadel Press Book
Published by Carol Publishing Group

Editorial Offices
600 Madison Avenue
New York, NY 10022

Sales & Distribution Offices
120 Enterprise Avenue
Secaucus, NJ 07094

In Canada: Musson Book Company
A division of General Publishing Co. Limited
Don Mills, Ontario

Manufactured in the United States of America
ISBN 0-8065-1109-5
10 9 8 7 6 5 4 3 2

Library of Congress Cataloging-in-Publication Data

Birren, Faber, 1900-
        The symbolism of color / by Faber Birren.
            p.   cm.
        Bibliography: p.
        ISBN 0-8065-1099-4.   ISBN 0-8065-1109-5 (pbk.)
        Color--Miscellanea. 2. Symbolism. 3. Occultism. 4. Psychical
    research. I. Title.
    BF1623.C6B53   1988   88-16208
    133--dc19   CIP

Contents

The
Symbolism
of
COLOR

Introduction

As the author (and compiler) of this book, let me tell of my interests and attitudes. As a young man I became fascinated with all aspects of occultism and mysticism, read and collected books on the subject, practiced crystal gazing, yoga and meditation, sat in semi-darkness to see human auras (unsuccessfully), and otherwise gave myself to the esoteric, short of joining a coven of witches.

I was employed by a publisher of books on the occult and on spiritualism. Through good fortune I met Houdini who at the time was devoting himself to an exposé of spiritualists. For him I assembled works on magic and the supernatural. During one winter I lent assistance to one of his agents (a woman dressed in black), my job being to go separately to spiritual meetings, making sure that I sat next to her at seances so one of her hands would be free. With a court stenographer, I later covered a mass meeting of spiritualists who were protesting Houdini's coming visit to Chicago to attack them.

This quite delightful interlude, if it did not extinguish my concern with things psychic, at least helped to temper my credulity in the metaphysical with a measure of gravity. If I gave myself to

7

things esoteric, I would henceforth keep one foot on the ground.

My efforts in the field of color quite naturally brought me in contact with scientists, and American scientists in particular, *in those days,* tended to disdain things occult. This became a source of irritation to me, for I saw no reason why I, or anyone else, couldn't accept and believe in phenomena which had no pat explanation. I admired the writings of Charles Fort, an Englishman who had devoted a lifetime to the collection of *data* which were inexplicable to science.

I introduced a word into my vocabulary—phlogiston—and injected it into conversations with skeptics. (Phlogiston was the term used by scientists in the 17th century as the supposedly material substance that enabled things to burn. It was, of course, a word only and no substance at all.) In effect, if there was nonsense in the occult, there was phlogiston in science.

My interest in mysticism continued to be nourished by me. In becoming a color consultant, I sedulously gathered any and all curiosities that related to color. In the preparation of a book called *The Story of Color,* portfolios of notes were assembled on man's concept of the universe, his religion, healing, culture, mythology, astrology, alchemy—plus anything human and unique to be found within the recognized sciences of physics, chemistry, biology, physiology, psychology.

The Story of Color was later reworked and republished with the title, *Color—A Survey in Words and Pictures.* (Other topics than mysticism were, of course, included.) Then came a highly successful book of mine, *Color Psychology and Color Therapy.* This was revised once and reprinted several times. It is still available in bookstores after 30 years!

All the while I have pursued the subjects included in this present book. My studies have had useful application in my profession as a color consultant, especially as to psychological effects. In developing color plans for neuropsychiatric facilities, for the mentally disturbed and mentally retarded, for the treatment of alcoholism and drug addiction, a sympathy for the emotional and psychic troubles of people has served me in good stead.

With the greatest of pleasure I have seen the mystic win victories in once esoteric realms such as the human aura, ESP, faith healing, precognition, and color therapy with visible light. The benefits of meditation, of biofeedback, measurements of body responses and brain waves, all much concerned with color, have worked their way into accepted medical and psychological practice.

What is happening these days is that rational science is no longer insisting on yes or no, black or white, factual answers for numerous phenomena. Things occult must be regarded, whether there can be proof or not. I wonder how many physicists know that Sir Isaac Newton wrote over a million words on religion, with the hope that science might one day lead to a better understanding of God. Religion itself is occult. Yet many who firmly believe in God may deny or reject psychic phenomena—a paradox indeed.

Stanley R. Dean has written, "A new age is dawning—the Psychic Age—on the heels of the Atomic Age and Space Age." He recommends that psychic research be recognized as a practical subject, be offered in universities, and that doctorates and degrees in it be awarded. Today, fortunately, funds are being set aside for such research, by governments, private industries, medical centers, universities, colleges, and other agencies.

Here I am in the middle with this book. The mystic may think me too skeptical, and the skeptic may think me too mystical. The middle is where I prefer to be, hopeful that former conflicts will be resolved and that the beauty and magic of color will not only enthrall man, as before, but become a more essential and vital part of his life.

—FABER BIRREN

I

Concepts of the Earth
and the Universe

When I wrote *The Story of Color* many years ago I did extensive
scholarly research on ancient traditions and symbolism. Much of
what I found out and had to say is included in the early chapters
of this present book. One discovery became clear at the very
beginning: the ancient use of color was by no means guided by
esthetics but by mysticism. Let me skip about in man's concept of
the earth and the universe (and himself) by referring to early historic records.

On the matter of race, for example, Charles Darwin in his *Descent of Man* wrote, "We know . . . that the color of the skin is
regarded by the men of all races as a highly important element in
their beauty." Perhaps one of the first indications that color
became a functional and symbolic art rather than a purely esthetic
one is to be found in this adoration of racial purity which was
distinguished by color purity. Extreme whiteness of skin among
northern peoples, extreme yellowness or goldness among Orientals, extreme blackness among Negroes became emblems of the
ideal racial type.

11

The ancient Egyptians recognized four races. They were of the red race and extremely proud of it to judge from their frequent application of red dye on their flesh. The hue yellow symbolized the Asiatic peoples. White was the color of the peoples to the north, across the Mediterranean and in parts of Asia Minor. Black was the hue of the Negro.

Following the Egyptians the Aryans also divided mankind into these four races. In India four castes were founded upon the same distinctions. The Arabs, however, accepted two races, one red or ruddy, the other black. In African mythology the descendants of those who ate the lungs and blood of the first ox slaughtered for food established the red race. Those who feasted on the liver begat the black.

Another interpretation is found in "The Tale of the Ensorcelled Prince" from the *Arabian Nights*. The evil wife of the Prince casts this spell upon the inhabitants of the Black Islands: "And the citizens, who were of four different faiths, Moslem, Nazarene, Jew and Magian, she transformed by her enchantments into fishes; the Moslems are the white, the Magians red, the Christians blue, and the Jews yellow."

Among American Indians one encounters the charming statement, "The morning star is like a man: he is painted red all over; that is the color of life." Dawn people dressed in red. Gold was sunlight, and the magic bridge from earth to heaven was the rainbow.

In mysticism the sun is dominant, and color was associated with it. Light was the greatest of all mysteries. The rays of the sun created and sustained all living things. Blackness was cold and foreboding. Color was vital to life because light ruled over life. And color was the crowning glory of light. In the Zoroastrian Scriptures one reads: "We sacrifice unto the undying, shining, swift-horsed Sun. When the light of the sun waxes warmer, when the brightness of the sun waxes warmer, then up stand the heavenly Yazatas, by hundreds and thousands: they gather together its glory, they make its glory pass down, they pour its glory upon the earth made by Ahura, for the increase of the world of holiness, for the increase of the creatures of holiness, for the increase of the undying, shining, swift-horsed Sun."

It is obvious—and historic research will bear out the point—that color became part of the so-called Mysteries in the earliest stage of civilization. Knowledge of the unknown was the highest of arts. Such knowledge belonged to the elect, to those few souls who through some divine insight seemed best qualified to interpret the baffling secrets of nature and the supreme deity. They prescribed the symbolism of color that was to endure for so many centuries—modified here and there as one nation won ascendency over another, but remaining substantially the same up to modern times.

Evidence that the inspiring beauty of color had its origin in mysticism, in a sort of functional application of hue to interpret life and the world, *and not in esthetics,* piles high as one digs in the ruins of antiquity. Nearly every race and civilization had definite ideas about the colors of the cardinal points of the compass. For example, among the peoples of Tibet in Central Asia the world was conceived as being a high mountain. This the Mongols called Sumur. From the beginning of time the earth grew. Its summit rose to a height beyond the reach of man and hence provided a convenient dwelling place for the gods. An old legend relates: "In the beginning was only water and a frog, which gazed into the water. God turned this animal over and created the world on its belly. On each foot he built a continent, but on the navel of the frog he founded the Sumur Mountain. On the summit of this mountain is the North Star."

This mountain was shaped like a pyramid with its top broken off. The sides facing the four points of the compass were hued and shone like jewels. To the north was yellow, to the south blue, to the east white, to the west red. In each of these directions was a continent within a salty sea. The continents and the isles that stood about them had shapes to resemble the faces of the people who dwelt upon them. The people to the south, India, China, Mongolia, had oval faces. Those to the north had square faces. Those to the west had round faces. The faces of those to the east were crescent-shaped.

In China there were four heavenly kings who maintained guard over the four directions of the world.

Mo-li Shou, the guardian of the north, had a black face. Within his bag was a creature that assumed the form of a snake or white winged elephant and devoured men.

Mo-li Hung, the guardian of the south, had a red face. He held the umbrella of chaos, at the elevation of which there was universal darkness, thunder and earthquakes.

Mo-li Shoo, guardian
of the north. His face
was black.

Mo-li Ch'ing, guardian
of the east. His face
was green.

Mo-li Hair, guardian of
the west. His face was
white.

Mo-li Hung, guardian
of the south. His face
was red.

The four Heavenly Kings of China. They maintained guard over the four
directions of the world.

Mo-li Ch'ing, the guardian of the east, had a green face. His expression was ferocious and his beard like copper wire. With his magic sword, "The Blue Cloud," he caused a black wind which produced tens of thousands of spears to pierce and destroy the bodies of men.

Mo-li Hai, the guardian of the west, had a white face. At the sound of his guitar all the world listened and the camps of the enemies took fire.

Color symbolism for the points of the compass is to be found in lands as far removed from each other as Egypt and Ireland, China, and America. The ancient and the primitive respected them. They were observed in the construction of temples and altars, in rites and ceremonies.

In America these color associations existed in the mythology of practically every Indian tribe. Thousands of years ago, according to one fable, the Navahos dwelt in a land surrounded by high mountains. The rise and fall of these mountains created day and night. The eastern mountains were white and caused the day. The western mountains were yellow and brought twilight. The northern mountains were black and covered the earth in darkness, while the blue mountains to the south created dawn.

A further delightful Navaho legend is found in *The Mythology of All Races.* "First Man and First Woman, Black Body and Blue Body, built the seven mountains of the Navaho land, one at each cardinal point, and three in the centre. Through Tsisnadzini in the east, they ran a bolt of lightning to fasten it to earth. They decorated it with white shells, white lightning, white corn, dark clouds, and he-rain. They set a big bowl of shell on its summit, and in it they put two eggs of the Pigeon to make feathers for the mountain. The eggs they covered with a sacred buckskin to make them hatch. All these things they covered with a sheet of daylight, and they put the Rock-Crystal Boy and the Rock-Crystal Girl into the mountain to dwell."

Other legends are then related. "Mount Taylor, of the San Mateo range, is the southern mountain, and this was pinned to earth with a great stone knife, adorned with turquoise, mist, and she-rain, nested with bluebird's eggs, guarded by Turquoise Boy and Corn Girl, and covered with a blanket of blue sky. San Francisco, in Arizona, the mountain of the west, was bound with a sunbeam, decked with haliotis shell, clouds, he-rain, yellow maize and animals, nested with eggs of the Yellow Warbler, spread with yellow cloud, and made the home of White-Corn Boy and Yellow-Corn Girl. San Juan, in the north, was fastened with a rainbow, adorned with black beads, nested with eggs of the Blackbird, sheeted with darkness, and made the abode of Pollen Boy and Grasshopper Girl."

The American Indian also had color designations for a lower world which was generally black and an upper world which had many colors. All this symbolism was a part of his art. The tattooing on his face, the colors on his masks, effigies, huts were full of meaning and not mere products of an artistic temperament. He applied these hues of the compass to his songs, ceremonies, prayers, and games. Even today the Hopi in executing a dry-painting is a mystic before he is an artist. Religiously he places his yellow color first which represents the north. Then, in order, he places the green or blue of the west, the red of the south, and lastly the white of the east.

The art of color has a heritage such as this. Seldom did the ancient indulge in emotional fancy with hues, except to use those recognized by the Mysteries. His art was full of definitions. To the Indian, red symbolized day and black symbolized night—always. Red, yellow, and black were masculine colors; white, blue, and green were feminine. Certain tribes related hues to the four Indian elements, fire, wind, water, and earth. To the Cherokee, red signified success and triumph. Blue denoted tribulation and defeat. White stood for peace and happiness, black for death. Prayer sticks were bright with green to call the rain and livid with red before the war. In Tibet the very moods of humans had a mystical relationship to color. White and yellow complexions portrayed a mild nature. Red, blue, and black portrayed a fierce nature. Light blue was celestial. Gods were white, goblins red, devils black.

As with the earth and the points of the compass, the mystic of old identified color with matter itself. The concept of the world as comprised of simple elements is perhaps as old as mankind. One of the first of such references is to be found in the Hindu *Upanishads,* which date back to the seventh or eighth century B.C.: "Of all living things there are indeed three origins only, that which springs from an egg, that which springs from a living being, and that which springs from a germ. . . .

"The red color of burning fire is the color of fire, the white color of fire is the color of water, the black color of fire the color of earth. Thus vanishes what we call fire, as a mere variety, being a name, arising from speech. What is true is the three colors. The red color of the sun is the color of fire, the white of water, the black of earth. Thus vanishes what we call the sun, as a mere variety, being a name, arising from speech. What is true is the three colors. The red color of the moon is the color of fire, the white of water, the black of earth. Thus vanishes what we call the moon, as a mere variety, being a name, arising from speech. What is true is the three colors. The red color of the lightning is the color of fire, the white of water, the black of earth. Thus vanishes what we call the lightning, as a mere variety, being a name, arising from speech. What is true is the three colors. . . .

"Great householders and great theologians of olden times who knew this have declared the same, saying, 'No one can henceforth mention to us anything which we have not heard, perceived, or known.' Out of these they knew all. *Whatever they thought looked red, they knew was the color of fire. Whatever they thought looked white, they knew was the color of water. Whatever they thought looked black, they knew was the color of earth.* Whatever they thought was altogether unknown, they knew was some combination of those three beings." (The italics are mine.)

Color symbols for the elements have been variously chosen. The Jewish historian Josephus associated white with earth, purple with water, red with fire, and yellow with air. Leonardo da Vinci decided that earth was yellow, water was green, fire red, and air blue.

In Asia the Chinese recognized five elements—earth, water, fire, wood, and metal. C.A.S. Williams in his *Outlines of Chinese Symbolism,* a remarkable book originally published at Peiping and rich with stories and pictures of Chinese lore, writes: "Upon these five elements or perpetually active principles of Nature the whole scheme of Chinese philosophy . . . is based." The colors of the elements were also primary. Earth was yellow. Water was black. Fire was red. Wood was green. Metal was white.

Water produced wood but destroyed fire.

Fire produced earth but destroyed metal.

Metal produced water but destroyed wood.

Wood produced fire but destroyed earth.

Earth produced metal but destroyed water.

To the ancient Chinese, man himself was a product of the elements, composed of yellowness and earth, blackness and water, redness and fire, greenness and wood, whiteness and metal. He is described in all his curious make-up in the following quotation from an ancient Chinese tome, the *Visuddhi-Magga:*

"The amount of the earthy element in the body of a man of medium size is about a bushel, and consists of an exceedingly fine and impalpable powder. This is prevented from being dispersed and scattered about abroad, because it is held together by about half a bushel of the watery element and is preserved by the fiery element and is propped up by the windy element. And thus prevented from being dispersed and scattered abroad, it masquerades in many different disguises, such as the various members and organs of women and men, and gives the body its thinness, thickness, shortness, firmness, solidity, etc.

"The watery element is of a juicy nature and serves to hold the body together. It is prevented from trickling or flowing away, because it rests in the earthy element and is preserved by the fiery element and is propped up by the windy element. And thus prevented from trickling or flowing away, it gives the body its plumpness and leanness.

"The fiery element has heat as its characteristic, and has a vaporous element, and digests what is eaten and drunk. Resting in the earthy element and held together by the watery element and propped up by the windy element, it cooks the body and gives it its beauty of complexion. And the body thus cooked is kept free from decay.

"The windy element is characterized by its activeness and its ability to prop up, and courses through every member of the body. Resting in the earthy element and held together by the watery element and preserved by the fiery element, it props up the body. And it is because the body is thus propped up that it does not fall over, but stands upright. And it is when the body is impelled by the wind element that it performs its four functions of walking, standing, sitting or lying-down, or draws in and stretches out its arms, or moves its hands and its feet.

"Thus does this machine made up of the four elements move like a puppet, and deceives all foolish people."

Most peoples of the world had legends related to different ages. Mostly evil drove men from heaven to earth where they encountered no end of problems. The following tale appears in *The Mythology of All Races.*

The Greek poet Hesiod relates that in the beginning the Olympians under Kronos created the race of the Men of Gold. In those days men lived like gods in unalloyed happiness. They did not toil with their hands, for earth brought forth her fruits without their aid. They did not know the sorrows of old age, and death was to them like passing away in a calm sleep. After they had gone hence, their spirits were appointed to dwell above the earth, guarding and helping the living.

"The gods next created the Men of Silver, but they could not be compared in virtue and happiness with the men of 'the elder age of golden peace.' For many years they remained mere children, and as soon as they came to the full strength and stature of manhood they refused to do homage to the gods and fell to slaying one another. After death they became the good spirits who live within the earth.

"The Men of Bronze followed, springing from ash-trees and having hearts which were hard and jealous, so that with them 'lust and strife began to gnaw the world.' All the works of their hands were wrought in bronze. Through their own inventions they fell from their high estate and from the light they passed away to the dark realm of king Hades unhonoured and unremembered.

"Zeus then placed upon earth the race of the Heroes who fought at Thebes and Troy, and when they came to the end of life the Olympian sent them to happy abodes at the very limits of the earth."

THE SUN .

II

Concepts of Heaven, Gods and Men

Man has always been convinced that his destiny upon earth is ruled by some divine power within the sky. Both the little universe of the microcosm and the great universe of the world were parts of an elaborate scheme. Heaven created all. Everything in existence once came out of nothingness and out of darkness. These were the extremes.

One of the most august mysteries was thus the sun. In the sun man recognized the majestic forces of heat and light. It was master of heaven and earth, creating and sustaining life, controlling the elements, the drought and the rain.

The sun became the principle of good, personified in the gods of all nations. To the Egyptian it was Ra, Athom, Amun, Osiris. To the Persian it was Mithras. To the Hindu it was Brahma. To the Chaldean it was Bel. To the Greek it was Adonis and Apollo.

In the earliest of times the sun was often personified as a beautiful youth with golden locks. This god was slain by the evil of the world and later restored by certain rituals and ceremonies of regeneration. Later the sun had other personifications. The

21

Egyptians, Assyrians, and Babylonians knew it as a sacred bull. Its hue was generally red, white, yellow or gold. Yet in India the true color was thought to be blue. The orange rays seen upon earth were the result of the diffusion of substances from the illusionary world.

Mostly the sun was likened unto a flaming ball of gold. This precious metal was in fact thought to be crystallized sunlight. It was adopted for the ornaments of priests and the crowns of kings. And gold was yellow like the solar orb itself.

All knowledge was with the gods who dwelt in the sky. Man therefore looked to the sky, to the sun, the planets and stars for his wisdom. To comprehend the harmony here was to solve all his mortal problems.

The earliest astrologers were Asiatics, and among these the Chaldeans were eminent. Over two thousand years before Christ astrology was an important science known to the magician and practiced to regulate the affairs of men. (Astrology will be discussed in a separate chapter.) Once again color had its pristine role in symbolizing mysterious things and forming taste in the arts.

Much of early architecture, for example, involved color symbolism of the sun and planets. Many years ago Dr. C. Leonard Woolley in the joint expedition of the British Museum and the Museum of Pennsylvania unearthed the ancient *ziggurat,* the "Mountain of God," at Ur between Bagdad and the Persian Gulf, one of the oldest buildings in the world. Dating back to 2300 B.C. it was thought to be the original home of Abraham and founded before the Flood.

The tower measured 200 feet in length, 150 feet in width, and was originally about 70 feet high. It was built in four stages, a great solid mass of brickwork. Woolley found an absence of straight lines. Horizontal planes bulged outward, vertical planes were slightly convex—a subtlety once thought to be of Greek origin and quite evident in the Parthenon.

The lowest stage of the tower was black, the uppermost red. The shrine was covered with blue glazed tile, the roof with gilded metal. Woolley writes, "These colors had mystical significance and stood for the various divisions of the universe, the dark underworld, the habitable earth, the heavens and the sun."

More pretentious *ziggurats,* have been unearthed. In the fifth

Building of the Tower of Babel according to Genesis XI. The tower had seven stages, each in a different color. From an old German engraving.

century B.C., Herodotus wrote of Ecbatana: "The Medes built the city now called Ecbatana, the walls of which are of great size and strength, rising in circles one within the other. The plan of the place is, that each of the walls should out-top the one beyond it by the battlements. The nature of the ground, which is a gentle hill, favors this arrangement in some degree, but it is mainly effected by art. The number of the circles is seven, the royal palace and the treasuries standing within the last. The circuit of the outer wall is very nearly the same with that of Athens. On this wall the battlements are white, of the next black, of the third scarlet, of the fourth blue, of the fifth orange; all these are colored with paint. The last two have their battlements coated respectively with silver and gold. All these fortifications Deïoces had caused to be raised for himself and his own palace."

Herodotus, to all indications, referred to the great temple of Nebuchadnezzar at Barsippa, the Birs Nimroud. Uncovered in modern times, its bricks bear the stamp of the Babylonian monarch who apparently rebuilt it in the seventh century B.C. It was 272 feet square at its base and rose in seven stages, each stage being set back away from a central point. Of this building James Fergusson writes, "This temple, as we know from the decipherment of the cylinders which were found on its angles, was dedicated to the seven planets or heavenly spheres, and we find it consequently adorned with the colors of each. The lower, which was also richly panelled, was black, the color of Saturn; the next orange, the color of Jupiter; the third red, emblematic of Mars; the fourth yellow, belonging to the Sun; the fifth and sixth, green and blue respectively, as dedicated to Venus and Mercury, and the upper probably white, that being the color belonging to the Moon, whose place in the Chaldean system would be upper-most."

Now as to gods, most ancient religions were founded on the myth of an omnipotent power within the sky. Famous in Egyptian mythology were the gods Osiris, his wife and sister Isis, and their son Horus. Osiris represented the material aspect of solar divinity and his color was green like the earth. An ancient Egyptian text says, "O Osiris, paint thyself with this wholesome offering—two bags of green paint."

Isis, the virgin of the world, is one of the most venerable of all mythological figures. She represented the principle of natural fecundity. Her symbol was the moon. Her child Horus, likened to the human race, was born of sun and moon, of the masculine and feminine principles of the universe encountered in the lore of all peoples throughout the world.

The beauty of Isis is described by Apuleius in this rather lengthy but eloquent description: "In the first place, then, her most copious and long hairs, being gradually intorted, and promiscuously scattered on her divine neck, were softly defluous. A multiform crown, consisting of various flowers, bound the sublime summit of her head. And in the middle of the crown, just on her forehead, there was a smooth orb resembling a mirror, or rather a white refulgent light, which indicated that she was the moon. Vipers rising up after the manner of furrows, environed the crown on the right hand and on the left, the Cerealian ears of corn were also extended from above. Her garment was of many colors, and woven from the finest flax, and was at one time lucid with a white splendor, at another yellow from the flower of crocus, and at another flaming with a rosy redness. But that which most excessively dazzled my sight, was a very black robe, fulgid with a dark splendor, and which, spreading round and passing under her right side and ascending to her left shoulder, there rose protuberant like the center of a shield, the dependent part of the robe falling in many folds, and having small knots of fringe, gracefully flowing in its extremities. Glittering stars were dispersed through the embroidered border of the robe, and through the whole of its surface: and the full moon, shining in the middle of the stars, breathed forth flaming fires. Nevertheless, a crown, wholly consisting of flowers and fruits of every kind, adhered with indivisible connection to the border of that conspicuous robe, in all its undulating motions. What she carried in her hands also consisted of things of a very different nature. For her right hand, indeed, bore a brazen rattle through the narrow lamina of which bent like a belt, certain rods passing, produced a sharp triple sound, through the vibrating motion of her arm. An oblong vessel, in the shape of a boat, depended from her left hand, on the handle of which, in that part in which it was conspicuous, an asp raised its erect head and largely swelling neck. And shoes woven from the leaves of the victorious palm tree covered her immortal feet."

There is much color symbolism here. The green color refers to the robe of nature. The black represents death, corruption, and degeneration. White, yellow, and red signify the eternal pagan trinity of sunrise, day, and dusk; of birth, life, and death; of body, mind, and spirit (the trinity of the Christians was blue, yellow, and red).

Like Isis, all other Egyptian gods were hued. Horus, the son of Isis, and the god of the south, of time, hours, days, and the narrow span of mortal existence was a white god, though sometimes depicted as red through the blood of his mother. He was said to come from the land of the four greens, a reference to the four lakes that were the source of the Nile.

Set, the deity of the north, of evil and darkness who made life miserable for gods and men, who mutilated Osiris, swallowed Isis and slew Horus, was black.

Shu who separated the earth from the sky was red.

Amen the god of life and reproduction was blue.

Yellow represented corn and was the hue assigned to Neith.

The color of Num was green.

Hek, the god of magic, had yellow skin.

Asar-Hopi, known to the Greeks as Serapis, is said to have been hewn in one effigy from a solid piece of emerald. Clement of Alexandria described a statue compounded of gold, lead, silver, tin, with sapphires, emeralds, and topazes ground down and mixed to form an indigo hue.

In Egypt, red or brown animals symbolized Sêth. In Egyptian paintings, women and sometimes persons from other lands were represented as having yellow bodies. Many sacred animals were black.

One Egyptian legend of the destruction of the human race declares, "Once there reigned on earth Râ', the god who shines, the god who had formed himself. After he had been ruler of men and gods together, the men plotted against him at a time when His Majesty—life, welfare, health—had grown old. His bones were of silver, his members of gold, his hair of genuine lapis lazuli."

The Egyptians, incidentally, dreaded red or pinkish brown cats. Cats with mixed coats of black, white, brown, were less remarkable. The black cat had great powers. Sailors always were sure to have one on their ship to foretell the weather.

After Egypt and Asia Minor came Greece. Unfortunately the

story of color in Greek and Roman mythology must be written mainly from literary sources—references to hue are exceedingly scarce. As mystics and artists the Greeks differed greatly from the Egyptians. Archaeological remains from the dry climate of the Nile valley still are fresh with hue. The colors of gods, the symbols of religion are well preserved in temple, tomb, and papyrus.

In Greece, however, time and climate have destroyed evidence that would be so interesting today. Contrary to popular belief, Greek sculpture and architecture once were colored and in brilliant hues that were functionally employed to symbolize the mystic principles of the universe. In this respect the art of color in Greece was little different from that of Africa, Asia, or elsewhere. After all, Greek learning came out of Egypt, Chaldee, and India, where color had played such a vital role.

When the Greeks presented Homer's *Odyssey,* they wore purple to signify the sea-wanderings of Ulysses. When acting in the *Iliad* they were clothed in scarlet, which was emblematic of the bloody encounters mentioned in the poem.

Athena, wise in the industries of peace and the arts of war, represented union with the mind of Zeus, the chief of the Olympian gods. She wore a robe called the *peplus.* This was golden in color and woven with figures of the gods conquering the giants. An emerald was upon her breastplate to mark her divine and enduring wisdom.

The red poppy was sacred to Ceres, the goddess of the harvest, and she was often portrayed ornamented with a garland of them about her neck.

The face of the wine-god Dionysus was sometimes painted red.

Iris, the goddess of the rainbow and the cupbearer of the gods, was clothed in many bright hues.

The priests of the temple wore white garments, and in Rome on the first of the new year the consul in a white robe and mounted on a white horse ascended the capitol to celebrate the triumph of Jupiter.

There are a number of Greek myths that concern color. When the handsome Adonis, loved by Aphrodite, was slain by a wild boar on Mount Lebanon, the river that ran down turned red. And when Aphrodite hastened to her wounded lover, she ran through bushes of white roses, the thorns of which tore her flesh. As a consequence, her blood dyed the "white roses forever red."

Let me now offer a few miscellaneous references to colors and gods. The Romans often reddened the faces of their gods with vermilion. Purple as the imperial color of Rome traces through Greece. It became the royal hue of the Caesars. Richard Payne Knight says, "The bodies of Roman Consuls and Dictators were painted red during the sacred ceremony of the triumph, and from this custom the imperial purple of later ages is derived." The emperor in his purple robes embroidered or spangled with gold was the personification of Jupiter. His chariot was drawn by white horses. In his right hand he carried a branch of laurel, in his left an ivory sceptor topped with an eagle. A wreath of laurel was upon his head. His face was reddened with vermilion. Over him a slave held a crown fashioned of gold to resemble oak leaves.

The ancient Druids of Britain saw magic in the spectrum. The culture established here antedated the Roman conquest. These people built temples to the sun and had gods that resembled those of the Mediterranean nations.

Eliphas Levi writes: "The Druids were priests and physicians, curing by magnetism and charging amulets with their fluidic influence. Their universal remedies were mistletoe and serpent's eggs, because these substances attracted astral light in a special manner."

At the head of the Druidic Order was the Arch-Druid. He wore a tiara to represent the sun's rays. His breastplate possessed mysterious powers and would strangle anyone making a false statement while wearing it. On the front of his belt was a magic brooch of white stone. With this the fire of the gods could be drawn from heaven.

At certain seasons the Druids climbed the oak tree and cut the mistletoe with a golden sickle. The mistletoe was then caught in a white robe, lest it be desecrated by contact with the earth. Usually a white bull was sacrificed under the tree.

The school of the Druids had three divisions. The lowest division was that of Ovate, an honorary degree requiring no special preparation. The Ovates wore green, the Druidic hue of learning, and were expected to be versed in medicine and astrology.

The second division was that of Bard. Blue was now worn to represent harmony and truth. The members of this division memorized the sacred Druidic poetry and were often pictured with the primitive harp. The Bards were teachers, and those neophytes seeking entrance into the mysteries wore robes of blue, green, and white.

In the third division, white robes, symbolic of purity and the sun, were used. The members here were the Druids who ministered to the religious needs of the people.

Thus to the Druid green represented wisdom, blue represented truth, white was the supreme emblem of purity.

A Celtic folk tale tells of a Green Isle in which spirits were seen sometimes above and sometimes below the water. "Its people are deathless, skilled in magic; its waters restore life and health to mortals; there magic apples grow; and thither mortals are lured or wander by chance."

The Blue Tengri was god of heaven to the ancient Persians.

White gods in Siberia were friendly; black gods brought evil.

The early Lapps never wore blue near holy places, because Rutu, an evil demon who tortured the dead, often appeared in blue garments.

The Mexican god Huitzilopochtli was born carrying a blue shield and dart. His limbs were painted blue and his head was adorned with plumes.

To swing to the Orient, the Hindu Scriptures give many references to color. One of them quoted elsewhere, identified black with earth, white with water, and red with fire. Gold, however, was the vital hue, the supreme emblem. "The face of truth remains hidden behind a circle of gold. Unveil it, O god of light, so that I who love the true may see!"

Man himself had color as an essential part of his makeup. In the Hindu *Upanishads* one reads, "There are in his body the veins called Hita, which are as small as a hair divided a thousand-fold, full of white, blue, yellow, green, and red." And again, "Symmetry of form, beauty of color, strength and compactness of the diamond, constitute bodily perfection." The father of Svetaketu counseled, not without a sense of humor, "Man is like a pillow-case. The color of one may be red, that of another blue, that of a third black, but all contain the same cotton. So it is with man—one is beautiful, another is black, a third holy, a fourth wicked, but the divine One dwells within them all."

Among the Hindus the word *Brahma* signified universal power or the ground of all existence. Brahma, the god, is represented as a red or golden-hued figure with four heads, four arms, four legs—facing the four directions of the world. He is the first person and the father of a great trinity. Vishnu, the second person, clad in the yellow of universal understanding, is the preserver. Siva, the third person, the destroyer and reproducer who holds the phallic emblem, is black.

Brahmanism recognizes yellow as a sacred color. It is the hue of the robes of the child initiate and is the marriage color of India.

Green is described as the color of the horse with seven heads which drew Om, the Sun, across the sky. The epithet *blue,* addressed to the gods of India, refers to their origin within the sea.

The color of Buddha was yellow. "No sooner has he set his right foot within the city-gate than the rays of six different colors which issue from his body rose hither and thither over palaces and pagodas, and deck them, as it were, with the yellow sheen of gold, or with the colors of a painting." Again, "When he sat down he illumined the whole tree with his radiance." This radiance "lighted up the whole tree with a golden color." In one description, however, he lost his usual golden hue and became black while fasting.

Among the thirty-two marks of the superman attributed to Buddha, four concern hue:

"His complexion is like bronze, the color of gold. . . .

"The down of his body turns upward, every hair of it, blue-black in color like eye-paint, in little curling rings, curling to the right. . . .

"His eyes are intensely blue. . . .

"Between the eyebrows appears a hairy mole white and like soft cotton down. . . ."

In his description of evil Buddha drew upon the color red. "Inhabitants of a heaven of sensual pleasure wander about through the world, with hair let down and flying in the wind, weeping and wiping their tears away with their hands, and their clothes red and in great disorder." Red as an emblem of sin: Buddha himself wore it to ponder over the iniquities of mankind. "And the Blessed One, putting on a tunic of double red cloth, and binding on his girdle, and throwing his upper robe over his right shoulder, would go thither and sit down, and for a while remain solitary, and plunged in meditation."

Originally in India there were four castes: the Brahmans, the Kshatriyas, the Vaisyas, and the Sudras. As the story goes, mankind once comprised four races. From the mouth of the creator came the Brahmans. From his arms came the Kshatriyas. From his thighs came the Vaisyas. And from his feet came the Sudras. These were the four *varnas,* a word which means color in the Sanskrit language—the branding irons of caste.

The Brahmans were white. They were to study, to teach, to sacrifice for themselves, and to be priests to others. They gave alms and received alms. They were privileged and of the sacred class.

The Kshatriyas were red. They were to study but not to teach, to sacrifice for themselves but not to officiate as priest. They were to give but not to receive alms. Their class was militant, and they governed and fought the wars.

The Vaisyas were yellow. They were of the mercantile class. They were to study, sacrifice for themselves, give alms, cultivate the fields, breed cattle, trade, and lend money at interest.

The Sudras were black. They were of the servile class and were to obtain their livelihood by laboring for others. They might practice the useful arts, but they were not to study the holy Vedas.

The royal color of the Sung Dynasty (960-1127 A.D.) in China was brown. The Ming Dynasty (1368–1644) was green. The Ch'ing Dynasty (1644–1912) was yellow, when only the emperor was privileged to wear the hue.

And the officials of the emperor were known by their colors. Each of the grades was distinguished by a colored button worn on the top of a cap. The first rank was coral, then blue, purple, crystal, white, and gold. The grandsons of the emperor rode in purple sedans. The sedans of higher officials were blue, those of lower officials green.

Among other Chinese, the literati and educated persons of the realm affected deep purple. Respectable Chinese wore sober hues, soft blues, grays, browns. Men preferred deep blue and black. Pink, green, and blue were almost universally feminine. Blue, above all, was and still is the conventional hue for clothing in China.

As to the Arabian Mohammed, he is described as entering

Mecca wearing a black turban and bearing a black standard. This standard of Mohammed at first was adorned with the Roman Eagle. But the flag of the later caliphs was black and bore the white legend, "Mohammed is the Apostle of God."

Allah is the true God, and Mohammed is his prophet! Green, being symbolic of verdure, is associated with the World Mother. Those who claim to be descendants of the prophet, and those who have made a pilgrimage to Mecca, wear green turbans.

Though references to color in the Koran are few, they nevertheless are significant and express the passionate hopes and ideals of the Moslem. "As to those who believe and do good works . . . for them are prepared gardens of eternal abode, which shall be watered by rivers; they shall be adorned therein with bracelets of gold, and shall be clothed in green garments of fine silks and brocades, reposing themselves therein on thrones." For the evildoers, "Verily we have prepared . . . chains and collars, and burning fire." The vain and rich man would wither and turn yellow like his gold. And hell "shall cast forth sparks as big as towers, resembling yellow camels in color."

Mohammed speaks of the final day of judgment: "On the day of resurrection thou shalt see the faces of those who have uttered lies concerning God, become black." And again, "On that day the trumpet shall be sounded; and we will gather the wicked together on that day, having gray eyes." "The heaven shall become like molten brass, and the mountains like wool of various colors, scattered abroad by the wind." "The heavens shall be rent in sunder, and shall become red as a rose."

Yet the blessed with enter the kingdom. The Lord "shall cast on them brightness of countenance, and joy; and shall reward them, for their patient persevering, with a garden, and silk garments. They will repose on couches and eat fruit which grows everywhere about them." "Upon them shall be garments of fine green silk." "We will espouse them to fair damsels, having large black eyes" and "complexions like rubies."

There will be gardens "of a dark green," fountains, fruit trees, and pomegranates. "Therein shall they delight themselves, lying on green cushions and beautiful carpets."

Mohammed, like all prophets before him, thus used color to express the glory that awaited the virtuous. Green became the most sacred of hues to be worn solely by those of perfect faith.

Yet to convince his disciples that his fervor was as mortal as it was divine, he said, "Wherefore I swear by the redness of the sky at sunset." Men would be convinced by this, for red was the color of their blood. They would also understand the bounty of God when he said, "Dost thou not see that God sendeth down rain from the heaven, and that we thereby produce fruits of various colors? In the mountains also there are some tracts white and red, of various colors; and others are of deep black: and of men, and beasts, and cattle there are those whose colors are in like manner various."

One of the most significant traditions of the Mohammedan father concerns color. At Mecca is the sacred shrine of Caaba, a quadrangular structure that stands in the center of the mosque and which is visited by millions of pilgrims.

The Keblah was originally of a dazzling white and was seen from every part of the earth. It was brought direct from heaven by Gabriel and given to Abraham when he built the temple. For ages it shone as a visible sign of the omnipresence of Allah. But through the sins of men it became black. And every good Moslem since has prayed for its restoration to the divine whiteness that is of God.

Among the Indians of America color was an intimate part of religion. Like the races of Africa, Europe, and Asia the primitive American had a hue for the universal deity. The Mexicans, for example, gave the name Kan to a god who supported the sky. The word itself meant yellow. One easily comprehends the symbolism of the Indian's pipe, or Calumet. The smoke of fire reached to the sky and was seen by the gods. And even the gods smoked, for they built fires of petrified wood, used a comet for a flame, and blew clouds into the wind to be seen by man. The Calumet was the Indian's altar, its smoke a proper offering. And he almost invariably sought a red stone from which to make it. For the sun god was red, the underworld god black, and the fire god varicolored.

THE MOON .

III

The Cabala—Ten Globes of Luminous Color

The Cabala (Cabbala, Kabbalah), an esoteric system of mysticism, while little known today, was once popular among the mystics of the middle ages. It was held in reverence and practiced by Jews and Christians. While it reflects a certain paganism, its chief devotion was to the Bible and the Scriptures, assuming that sacred words, letters, numbers, and colors had occult significance. God was the source from which all of everything emanated. "The inscrutable Godhead fills and contains the universe."

Albert Pike wrote, "One is filled with admiration, on penetrating into the Sanctuary of the Cabala, at seeing a doctrine so logical, so simple, and at the same time so absolute. The necessary union of ideas and signs, the consecration of the most fundamental realities by the primitive characters; the Trinity of Words, Letters, and Numbers; a philosophy as simple as the alphabet, profound and infinite as the Word; theorems more complete and luminous than those of Pythagoras; a theology summed up by counting on one's fingers; an Infinite which can be held in the hollow of an infant's hand; ten ciphers and twenty-two letters, a

35

triangle, a square, and a circle—these are all the elements of the Cabala.''

Pike's description, however, is an oversimplification. Secret meanings in the Cabala are quite complex and difficult to understand. What is fascinating in this story of color and mysticism is the emphasis of the Cabala on the Tree of the Sephiroth illustrated separately in black and white on page 37.

While the origin of the Cabala is difficult to ascertain, certain mystics believe that Moses ascended Mount Sinai three times, once to receive the Tables of the Written Law, once to receive the Soul of the Lord, and a third time to be instructed in the mysteries of the Cabala, the Soul of the Soul of the Law. Another tradition is that the first principles were taught by God to His Angels who later transmitted them to Adam and thence to Noah and Abraham, David and Solomon.

In Cabalism God was symbolized in the Tree of the Sephiroth and its ten globes of shining light. "All Supreme Degrees and all Sephiroth are one, and God embraces all the Sephiroth."

The Tree was sometimes shown as a chart, or as related to the human figure. The material body, like that of the universe, was believed to be an expression of ten globes or spheres of colored light. Here one finds the Greek Microcosm of man, the little world in the image of the great world.

The ten globes of the Sephiroth formed a tree of luminous beauty arranged in three columns. To the left was the column of Strength. In the center was the column of Mildness, the reconciling power. To the right was the column of Wisdom and Beauty. The 22 connecting channels corresponded to the letters of the Hebrew alphabet. When the ten globes and the 22 channels were combined they were said to represent the 32 nerves that branch out from the Divine Brain.

Symbolism in the ten luminous globes of the Sephiroth had many associations. The mystics who held it sacred apparently felt the need to embrace much of the culture and "science" of the times.

Among the planets, for example, which were included in astrology, Kether, the Crown, symbolized the Empyrean, Chokmah the Primum Mobile, Binah the Firmament. Chesed was for Saturn, Geburah for Jupiter, Tiphereth for Mars, Netzach for the Sun, Hod for Venus, Jesod for Mercury, Malkuth for the Moon.

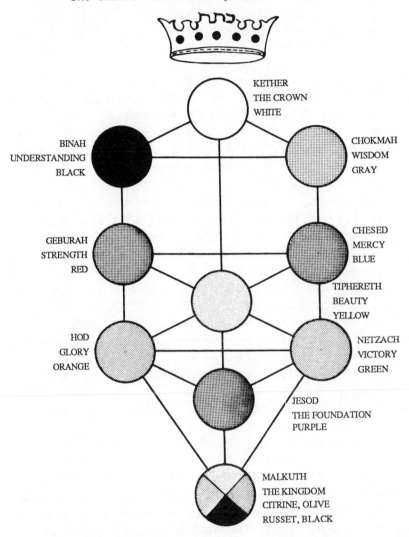

KETHER
THE CROWN
WHITE

BINAH
UNDERSTANDING
BLACK

CHOKMAH
WISDOM
GRAY

GEBURAH
STRENGTH
RED

CHESED
MERCY
BLUE

TIPHERETH
BEAUTY
YELLOW

HOD
GLORY
ORANGE

NETZACH
VICTORY
GREEN

JESOD
THE FOUNDATION
PURPLE

MALKUTH
THE KINGDOM
CITRINE, OLIVE
RUSSET, BLACK

The Sephiroth Tree of the Cabala. It was the chief symbol of an esoteric form of mysticism during the Middle Ages, revered alike by Christians and Jews. Its ten globes or spheres of colored light were a symbol of the glory of God and man.

In Alchemy, Kether represented mercury, Chokmah salt, Binah sulphur, these being the three principle elements of the alchemist. Chesed represented silver, Geburah gold, Tiphereth iron, Netzach tin, Hod copper, Jesod lead, and Malkuth "Water of Gold."

As to the Bible, the ten Sephiroth represented the ten names of God: Ehyeh, Yh, Jehovah, El the Mighty One, Eloah, Elohim, Jehovah Sabaoth, Elohim Sabaoth, El Hayy the Mighty Living One, Adonay the Lord. They also represented the Ten Classes of Angels and the Ten Members of the Human Body.

As to the body, Kether was associated with the head, Chokmah the brain, Binah the heart, Chesed the right arm, Geburah the left arm, Tiphereth the chest, Netzach the right leg, Hod the left leg, Jesod the genital organs, Malkuth the union of the whole body.

While the color symbolism of the ten Sephiroth varied with different writers and mystics of old, the separate illustration may be accepted as fairly representative. God the Cause of all things was the supreme, all-pervading source of "light." From Him came ten emanations to form the Tree of the Sephiroth. This Tree was likened unto man, the Microcosm. From God man received emanations which became his body, his understanding, mind, soul, and spirit. Through the twenty-two channels connecting the ten Sephiroth the whole was united to form one complete thing— all permeated by the might of God. The Tree was a symbol of the glory of God and man.

The color symbolism, therefore, is significant. Kether, the crown, the concentration of divine light is white. The Greeks, Druids, Confucianists, Shintoists, and Persians also conceived of white as the token of supreme divinity. This white of Kether formed a triad with Understanding and Wisdom. The symbol of Understanding (Binah) was black because it absorbed all light. The symbol of Wisdom (Chokmah) was thus gray, a blend of white and black.

These three Sephiroth formed a triad which led to a second triad of blue, red, and yellow. Here blue was the symbol of Mercy (Chesed), red the symbol of Strength (Geburah), and yellow the symbol of Beauty (Tiphereth).

From this second triad now came a third. The blue and yellow of Mercy and Beauty led to the green of Victory (Netzah). The red and yellow of Strength and Beauty led to the orange hue of Glory (Hod). The blue of Mercy and the red of Strength led to the purple of the "Foundation," (Jesod) the basis of all that was.

Finally, this triad of green, orange, and purple led to the tenth Sephiroth of the "Kingdom" (Malkuth). Here the hues were combined to form citrine, olive, russet, and black—a synthesis of *all* colors, ending in the ever-extinguishing black.

Thus was man the Microcosm, the little universe, fashioned in the likeness of God and born of His emanations. He would be worthy to reflect the glory of the great power that had created him.

JUDGEMENT.

IV

Jewish and
Christian Symbolism

In Jewish and Christian religious culture, color symbolism and mysticism also abound. As a prelude let me tell of Atlantis, the great mythical land described in majestic terms by Plato. Here dwelt a race of supermen who in time wandered over the earth and spread their culture to places as remote as Egypt, Chaldee, China, England, North and South America.

When the gods divided the earth, Poseidon was given the sea and the island continent of Atlantis. Magnificent cities were built of black and red stones. Each of the land zones had three walls, the outer one covered with brass, the middle one with tin, the inner one with orichalch, a yellowish metallic substance.

The capital of the central island was surrounded by a wall of gold. Poseidon's temple was covered with silver, its pinnacles with gold. The interior was of ivory, gold, and orichalch. Here the princes came, donned blue robes and renewed their oath before a sacred inscription carved on green stone.

The Atlantean theory is handy for reference when one wonders about the similarity of religious beliefs found in Asia and America, Africa, Europe and England, when scholars ponder over the incredibly perfect design of the Pyramids, the origin of Greek architectural styles, the amazing structures of Mexico and Central America. Then the blank chapters of history may be filled in with references to mythical Atlantis and its roving initiates.

One may even feel assured that the Garden of Eden and the city of the Golden Gates whose streets were paved with gold once existed and that the Flood of the Bible actually did destroy men for their iniquity.

According to an old Hebrew story, red, blue, purple, and white fire were collectively a symbol of the being of God. Red referred to love, sacrifice, and sin. Blue symbolized glory. Purple stood for splendor and dignity. White was the emblem of purity and joy.

Red, blue, purple, and white—they appear again and again throughout the Old Testament. The Lord commanded Moses to "Speak unto the children of Israel, that they bring me an offering: of every man that giveth it willingly with his heart ye shall take my offering. And this is the offering ye shall take of them: gold, and silver, and brass. And blue, and purple, and scarlet, and fine linen, and goats' hair, and rams' skins dyed red, and badgers' skins, and shittim wood, oil for the light, spices for anointing oil, and for sweet incense, onyx stones, and stones to be set in the ephod, and in the breastplate."

Blue, however, is predominantly the Lord's hue. In Exodus one reads, "Then up went Moses, and Aaron, and Nadab, and Abihu, and seventy of the elders of Israel; and they saw the God of Israel: and there was under his feet as it were a paved work of sapphire stone, and as it were the very heaven for clearness."

Ezekiel likened God unto a rainbow: "As the appearance of the bow that is in the cloud in the day of rain, so was the appearance of the brightness round about. This was the appearance of the likeness of the glory of the Lord." And Ezekiel continued, "And above the firmament that was over their heads was the likeness of a throne, as the appearance of a sapphire stone: and upon the likeness of the throne was the likeness as the appearance of a man above it. And I saw as the color of amber."

The throne of God was thus blue like sapphire, surrounded by a rainbow, and pierced by the golden hue of amber which apparently emanated from the Lord. And that the Lord preferred blue may be inferred from his command to Moses to "Speak unto the children of Israel, and bid them that they make them fringes in the borders of their garments, throughout their generations, and that they put upon the fringe of the borders a ribband of blue . . . that ye may remember, and do all my commands, and be holy unto your God.''

Much of the symbolism preserved to this day in the Jewish rite is to be found in Exodus, in the writings of Philo Judaeus and in *The Antiquities of the Jews* by Josephus. In the building of the tabernacle the Lord commanded, "Moreover thou shalt make the tabernacle with ten curtains of fine twined linen, and blue, and purple, and scarlet: with cherubims of cunning work shalt thou make them."

It is thus only natural that red, blue, purple, and white should become the divine hues of Judaism. Josephus, who lived in the first century A.D. and who was familiar with the mysticism of the Greeks and Romans, sought to ally the hues with the four elements. He wrote, "The veils, too, which were composed of four things, they declared the four elements; for the plain [white] linen was proper to signify the earth, because the flax grows out of the earth; the purple signified the sea, because that color is dyed by the blood of a sea shellfish; the blue is fit to signify the air; and the scarlet will naturally be an indication of fire."

Thus were the veils of the tabernacle given esoteric significance. Josephus then describes the vestments of the high priest and relates these also to the four elements of the ancient Greeks.

The priest wore several garments. First was a girdle which he fastened about his loins. Over this he wore a linen vestment which reached to the ground and had sleeves. About the breast was tied a girdle, "so loosely woven that you would think it were the skin of a serpent. It is embroidered with flowers of scarlet, and purple, and fine twined linen."

Upon his head he wore a cap made to resemble a crown. This was covered with linen.

Now the high priest "is indeed adorned with the same garments that we have described, without abating one; only over these he puts on a vestment of blue." This garment was a long robe that reached to the priest's feet. It was also tied with a girdle and embroidered with scarlet, blue, and purple. On the bottom of this was a fringe, "in color like pomegranates, with golden bells."

The final garment was the ephod. It was short and came slightly below the waist. It had sleeves and was embroidered in color, "but it left the middle of the breast uncovered."

Over the ephod in the center of the chest of the high priest was fixed the essen or breastplate. It was tied in place with blue ribbons attached to four golden rings. There were two sardonyxes on the shoulders of the ephod which served as buttons to hold the breastplate.

The breastplate itself had twelve stones, "extraordinary in largeness and beauty." These stood in four horizontal rows. In the first row were a sardonyx, a topaz, and an emerald. In the second row were a carbuncle, a jasper, and a sapphire. In the third row were a ligure, an amethyst, and an agate. In the fourth row were a chrysolite, an onyx, and a beryl. The names of the sons of Jacob were engraved on the gems, each representing one of the twelve tribes of Israel.

The high priest also wore a mitre which was colored and out of which rose a cup of gold described by Josephus in some detail. Referring to the Greek conception of the universe, he wrote: "Now the vestment of the high priest being made of linen, signified the earth; the blue denoted the sky, being like lightning in its pomegranates, and in the noise of the bells resembling thunder. And for the ephod, it showed that God had made the universe of four [elements]; and as for the gold interwoven, I suppose it related to the splendor by which all things are enlightened. He also appointed the breastplate to be placed in the middle of the ephod, to resemble the earth, for that has the very middle place of the world. And the girdle which encompassed the high priest round, signified the ocean, for that goes round about and includes the universe. Each of the sardonyxes declare to us the sun and the moon; those, I mean, that were in the nature of buttons on the high priest's shoulders. And for the twelve stones, whether we understand by them the months, or whether we understand the like number of the signs of that circle which the Greeks call the zodiac, we shall not be mistaken by their meaning. And for the mitre, which was of a blue color, it appears to mean heaven; for how otherwise could the name of God be inscribed upon it?"

Scholars have endeavored to reveal the meaning of these color symbols. The twelve gems of the breastplate were said to

The Jewish High Priest. He wore several garments of different hues,
including a crown of linen. On his breastplate were twelve precious
stones, engraved with the names of the sons of Jacob, and representing
the twelve tribes of Israel.

represent the twelve great qualities and virtues of illumination, love, wisdom, truth, justice, peace, equilibrium, humility, strength, faith, joy, victory.

Red was properly a token of love and sacrifice, of sin and salvation. In Isaiah one reads: "Come now, and let us reason together, saith the Lord: though your sins be as scarlet, they shall be white as snow; though they be red like crimson, they shall be as wool."

Blue, the main hue, predominant in the vestments of the high priest and used to wrap sacred vessels, referred to the glory of the Lord. Purple represented His divine condescension.

White signified purity and victory. Along with red, it implied that the priest was not only the servant of the God of love, but also of the God of anger.

Black, yellow, and green do not seem to have much religious sanction in the Old Testament, although the colors do appear in the New Testament and are included in the Roman Catholic Rite.

Through the centuries these hues have become a part of many traditions and legends. It is believed, for example, that the tablet given to Moses on Mount Sinai was fashioned of sapphire to indicate its divine origin. A red carbuncle as at the prow of Noah's ark—to spread light and guidance to the holy man. He was also shown the rainbow as a sign that peace was again upon the earth. The rainbow symbolized the unity of man and Deity, stretching as it did from earth to heaven and containing all hues. "And God said: This is the token of the covenant which I make between me and you, and every living creature that is with you, for perpetual generations. I do set my bow in the cloud, and it shall be for a token of a covenant between me and the earth. And it shall come to pass, when I bring a cloud over the earth, that the bow shall be seen in the cloud: and I will remember my covenant, which is between me and you, and every living creature of all flesh; and the waters shall no more become a flood to destroy all flesh."

Much of pagan and Jewish mysticism found its way into early Christianity, and into the New Testament itself. The crucifix had been familiar to the Egyptians and Babylonians and even to the Aztecs of America. In Greece the world had been symbolized by a cross, its four quarters embellished with a bull to signify earth, a scorpion to signify water, a lion to signify fire, and the human head to signify air.

The nimbus or halo of the saint had been used in Egypt, but as an expression of power rather than holiness. Likewise worship of the sun had led to the conception of the deity as a trinity, representing the three phases of dawn, midday, and dusk and the three periods of growth, maturity, and decay in life. The philosophers had also spoken of the past, the present, and the future; the body, mind, and spirit.

In the early days of Christianity the Trinity of God became associated with the colors blue, yellow, and red. God the Father was blue, God the Sun yellow, and God the Holy Ghost red. The Deity thus was symbolized by the triangle and the shamrock. In man the threefold aspect of his nature and being was expressed in the conception of his body as red, his mind yellow, and his spirit blue.

And heaven was blue, earth yellow, and hell red.

Further legends of a mystical nature grew with the rise of Christianity. One of these is the fascinating story of the Holy Grail. When Michael and his legions swooped down upon Lucifer his sword struck the green stone from the coronet of the rebellious one. It fell to earth and later was fashioned into the Holy Grail from which Christ is said to have drunk at the Last Supper. Later the cup was brought to the place of the Crucifixion and used to catch the blood pouring from the wounds of the Son of Man. It was then carried away to England. Finally, Parsifal, the last of the Grail Kings, carried the Holy Cup to India where it disappeared.

There was perhaps ample reason for the creation of such myths, for the New Testament itself was filled with esoteric writings. The Revelation of St. John the Divine concealed mysteries which prodded the superstitious minds of the people. In the Old Bible Zechariah had written, "I saw by night, and behold a man riding upon a red horse, and he stood among the myrtle trees that were in the bottom; and behind him there were red horses, speckled, and white." And later, "In the first chariot were red horses; and in the second chariot black horses. And in the third chariot white horses; and in the fourth chariot grisled and bay horses."

Then almost the same description had been given by St. John the Divine: "And I saw, and behold a white horse: and he that sat on him had a bow; and a crown was given unto him: and he went forth conquering, and to conquer.

"And there went out another horse that was red: and power was given to him that sat thereon to take peace from the earth, and that they should kill one another: and there was given unto him a great sword.

"And when he had opened the third seal, I heard the third beast say, Come and see. And I beheld, and lo a black horse; and he that sat on him had a pair of balances in his hand.

"And I looked, and behold a pale horse: and his name that sat on him was Death, and Hell followed with him. And power was given unto them over the fourth part of the earth, to kill with sword, and with hunger, and with death, and with the beasts of the earth."

Color symbolism in the New Testament and consequently in Christianity is not limited to a tetrad of red, blue, purple, and white as among the Jews. Green notably becomes significant and is called the hue of God. St. John the Divine writes, "And he that sat was to look upon like a jasper and a sardine stone: and there was a rainbow round about the throne, in sight like unto an emerald."

Among the hues of the spectrum, red was the symbol of charity and martyrdom for faith. It signified the Blood of Christ, and the martyr was clothed in it. Red became the color of the lamp flickering before the high altar, an everlasting reminder of the suffering and sacrifice of the Son of Man. In the familiar Christmas legend of the shepherd's daughter, the white rose she presented to the Infant turned red when He touched it and foretold His future suffering.

Gold and yellow represented power and glory. Here was the hue of the nimbus of the saint, the gates of heaven—and a reminder of the pompous glory of the golden cock, golden eagle, hawk, ass, calf.

Saffron was the hue of the confessors.

Green symbolized faith, immortality, and contemplation. It was everlasting like nature. The walls of the New Jerusalem were described as being made of green jasper. Saints were adorned with green robes to indicate their eternal life.

Pale green was the hue of baptism.

Blue signified hope, the love of divine works, sincerity and piety. It was the color assigned to the Virgin Mary and through it she entered the dominion of God.

Pale blue was symbolic of peace, serene conscience, Christian prudence, the love of good works.

Purple was emblematic of suffering and endurance. It was also the hue of the penitent. Christ was believed to have worn purple garments before His Crucifixion. In purple robes He is the self-sacrificing God. Martyrs wore purple, as did some old orders of nuns, as a sign of repentance and of devout faith in the compassion of the Saviour. Rosaries were frequently made of amethyst for all these reasons.

White represented chastity, innocence, and purity.

Black represented death and regeneration. The black rose was a symbol of silence among Christian initiates. "I will give thee the treasures of darkness."

Gray was an emblem of Christ risen, a blend of the divine light of creation and the darkness of sin and death.

Regenerated man is colorfully described in the *Song of Solomon.* "My beloved is white and ruddy, the chiefest among ten thousand. His head is as the most fine gold, his locks are bushy, and black as a raven. His eyes are as the eyes of doves by the rivers of waters, washed with milk, and fitly set. His cheeks are a bed of spices, as sweet flowers: his lips like lilies, dropping sweet smelling myrrh. His hands are as gold rings set with beryl: his belly is as bright ivory overlaid with sapphires. His legs are as pillars of marble, set upon sockets of fine gold: his countenance is as Lebanon, excellent as the cedars. His mouth is most sweet: yea, he is altogether lovely. This is my beloved, and this is my friend, O daughters of Jerusalem."

There is, finally, an impressive exaltation of color in St. John the Divine's vision of the New Jerusalem. He tells of a city rich with color, its twelve foundations garnished in order with jasper, sapphire, chalcedony, emerald, sardonyx, sardius, chrysolyte, beryl, topaz, chrysoprasus, jacinth, and amethyst. The twelve gates were pearls. The wall of the city was of jasper, the streets gold.

And here also is found one of the most magnificent of all descriptions of Christ:

"And I saw heaven opened, and behold a white horse; and he that sat upon him was called Faithful and True, and in righteousness he doth judge and make war.

"His eyes were as a flame of fire, and on his head were many crowns; and he had a name written, that no man knew, but he himself.

"And he was clothed with a vesture dipped in blood: and his name is called The Word of God.

"And the armies which were in heaven followed him upon white horses, clothed in fine linen, white and clean. . . .

"And he hath on his vesture and on his thigh a name written, KING OF KINGS, AND LORD OF LORDS."

V

Sorcery and Magic, Life and Death

Witchcraft has had a revival in the United States. Popular associations may be on the quaint side—the Halloween mask and costume, the witch riding on a broomstick. Plays and moving pictures may portray a capricious witch playing tricks among otherwise worldly people. Witches may be cavorting with ghosts, making things disappear and disappearing themselves. All in good fun.

But witchcraft has been and still is an ominous practice. Voodooism is witchcraft, and with its spells, charms, fetishes it strikes terror in many credulous souls. Yet witchcraft is also practiced among persons of intelligence and sophistication. Cults in America have engaged in dissolute practices that have led to the mutilation and killing of animals and to the murder of human beings. There is a devil; there is evil; and demons line up in mortal conflict with angels.

There is little of color associated with witchcraft, so in this book chief emphasis has been placed on sorcery and magic, which are more concerned with human salvation than destruction.

51

Witchcraft is by no means paganism, for it is quite mixed up with religion and Christianity. At Sabbaths, which were usually held in February, May, August, November (Halloween), pacts were made with the Devil. In Satanic rites, Jehovah, Christ, the Virgin might be denounced and the Bible and crucifix trampled under foot. Souls were bartered for worldly gain, unholy pacts made with the devil. There is the legend of Faust who gave his soul to Mephistopheles in exchange for youth, knowledge and magical power. There is Stephen Vincent Benét's *The Devil and Daniel Webster*. In the Bible, Saul consulted the Witch of Endor and bid her, "Bring me up Samuel." There are otherwise about 18 references to witchcraft in the Bible, mostly to forbid and abolish it. One declares, "Thou shalt not suffer a witch to live" (Exodus). In the 16th Century the French estimated that some 7,405,900 witches were wandering about. Martin Luther is said to have thrown an inkpot at Satan's head, and the blotch of ink still is visible in the room where the incident took place.

As is well known, witches were beaten, stoned, drowned, hanged and burned at the stake. As to color, the Devil was red, and witchcraft involved the Black Art, Black Book. Religions have rites and incantations to exorcise evil spirits and demons. Exorcisms were also needed to dislodge evil spirits hidden in food, wine, salt, houses, beds, ships.

Witches often took the form of dogs, cats, jackals, bulls, stags, toads. They could cause disease, plague, madness; turn milk sour, destroy harvests. To cover the mouth while yawning was to prevent a demon from invading the body. There must be protection against witches and witchcraft, and in this protection color assumed a truly major role. If the Christian could dispel the witch by raising a crucifix or making the sign of the cross, his more primitive brothers needed other devices.

Let me tell of the powers of color in foiling witches and in preserving a man from the ultimate of terrors—death. Primitive tribes throughout the world, the American Indian included with the tribes of Africa, Fiji, New Guinea, Australia, must be charmed against death. First the manslayer, having done away with his enemy, was in immediate danger of having the spirit of the dead man attack and slay him as well.

To make a world tour of manslayers, let me first describe the august appearance of the veteran Indian warrior of eastern

America in the 18th century. The description is from Heckewelder's book. "In the year 1742, a veteran warrior of the Lenape nation and Monsey tribe, renowned among his own people for his bravery and prowess, and equally dreaded by their enemies, joined the Christian Indians who then resided at this place. This man, who was then at an advanced age, had a most striking appearance, and could not be viewed without astonishment. Besides that his body was full of scars, where he had been struck and pierced by the arrows of the enemy, there was not a spot to be seen, on that part of it which was exposed to view, but what was tattooed over with some drawing relative to his achievements, so that the whole together struck the beholder with amazement and terror. On his whole face, neck, shoulders, arms, thighs and legs, as well as on his breast and back, were represented scenes of the various actions and engagements he had been in; in short, the whole of his history was there deposited, which was well known to those of his nation, and was such that all who heard it thought it could never be surpassed by man."

Such regal appearance no doubt impressed his friends and struck fright in his adversaries. And it perhaps safeguarded him also from the spirits of those he had dispatched.

In the Arctic Circle of America, a group of Indians, having killed an Eskimo, took precautions before their next meal. Thus: when food was cooked "all the murderers took a kind of red earth or ochre, and painted all the space between the nose and chin, as well as the greater part of their cheeks, almost to the ears, before they would taste a bit." (Frazer, *The Golden Bough*.)

In Africa, similar practices were common among various tribes. The Nandi after killing the member of another tribe painted one side of his body, spear and sword red, and the other side white. In the Congo, the slain man was sure to avenge his death in after-life by in turn slaying his murderer. To be protected, the manslayer applied the red tail-feathers of a parrot to his hair and painted his forehead red. In other tribes, when a war party returned to the village, the surviving victims were washed by the women with a mixture of fat and butter, and their faces were painted red and white.

The Masai of Africa painted half their bodies red and the other half white. The Wagogo of East Africa painted a red circle around his right eye and a black circle around his left eye. In other tribes, manslayers painted their faces white, and put white bands around their chests. Others roasted flesh, after which faces were blackened with the ashes of the fire. To complete the ritual, mouths were later rinsed with milk and brown paint restored to their bodies.

In Fiji, a native after clubbing a man to death was smeared from head to foot by the chief of his tribe.

In New Guinea, "When the relations of a murdered man have accepted a bloodwit instead of avenging his death, they must allow the family of the murderer to mark them with chalk on the brow. If this is not done, the ghost of their murdered kinsman may come and trouble them for not doing their duty by him; for example, he may drive away their swine or loosen their teeth." (Frazer, *The Golden Bough.*)

In Australia, some manslayers hold themselves safe from the spirit of the dead man by painting their faces and bodies in bright colors. In an interesting Australian practice, the manslayer is painted black to make him invisible to the ghosts of his enemies, but the widow of the deceased must paint herself white so her husband's spirit will know she is dutifully in mourning.

In 1976 the newspapers of Queensland, Australia, told of the ominous appearance of the Red Ochre Man, an Aboriginal from Camooweal, out to avenge the slaying of one of his tribesmen. Painted red from head to foot, carrying beads and rattles, his feet shod with feathers to avoid footprints, he was a demon of terror to those he sought—and to all aboriginals along his path. According to the press, "Word has been sent out to the two chaps he's supposed to be after to make tracks or at least stay out of town."

Perhaps the Red Ochre Man was a "dangerous fake." A tribal elder told that such ghouls did not paint themselves red until they actually confronted their victims. Nor did they drink wine or beg for food. How to tell the genuine from the pretender? A certain Mr. Assan challenged the Red Ochre Man to a fight with boomerangs, spears or gloves. He then called upon an "extraordinary" magician with Kadaitja powers. Meanwhile, "All the young fellas left when the Red Ochre Man arrived and they are not back yet."

There was danger also in the spirits of slain animals. In South Africa the lion-killer painted his body white, went into seclusion for four days, then returned to the village with his flesh painted

red. In West Africa, a more complex ritual followed the killing of
a leopard. First a procession was held and the dead leopard was
tied to a tree. The leopard-slayer then had one side of his body
painted with white and red to resemble the spots of the animal. A
basket in the same colors was attached to his head, and magical
strings were tied around his hands and feet. After this he crawled
about and roared like a leopard.

In British Columbia, after killing a bear the hunter painted his
face and the face of his fellow-hunters in alternate stripes of red
and black. If they failed to do this the spirit of the bear (a good
animal) and the spirits of all other bears would be offended.

On the inevitability of death, men needed to be constantly protected against the onslaught of demons and the spells of witches.
One great fear, dating back to ancient Egypt and ancient India
was the Evil Eye. One glimpse of it and a man was likely to be
cursed with misfortune, insanity, or disease. The evil eye was the
fabulous witch that went about wrecking the life, love, labor, and
sanity of men.

Some primitives wore round blue disks strung together with
beads and painted with the symbol of an eye. In Persia a bit of
turquoise was placed in the eye of a sacrificial lamb, the animal
roasted, and the stone then put in an amulet case and sewn into a
child's headdress.

Pliny states that the magicians once protected themselves with
jet. In India the Hindu mother put daubs of black on the nose and
forehead or on the eyelids of her babe. She also tied a piece of
white or blue cloth on her dress. In Jerusalem the "hand of
might," almost always blue, was worn as a bracelet. In Scotland
the new-born was made safe from the evil eye by a piece of red
ribbon tied about its neck. In parts of England a ring or amulet of
red chalcedony was worn. In Italy a piece of coral held the
needed power.

Another common and universal fear was of spells and of the
evil work of witches. Here colors, symbols, amulets were called
upon for defense. The ancient Egyptians charmed their lives with
a variety of amulets. The formulas of the magicians were often
written in red ink. This is true of the rites and ceremonies found
in the famous Egyptian *Book of the Dead*. Color had potent force
in the resistance of evil and the overthrow of demons. And where
it was a natural product of nature, permanently resisting fading,

as in precious and semi-precious stones, its power was supreme.

From Egyptian and Babylonian inscriptions it is known that amulets of certain gems and hues were thought to bless their wearer with the favor of the gods and bring them into daily contact with divine beings. Some of these stones had curious markings like veins. Others resembled eyes. They were to be worn next to the scalp or forehead, against the ear, heart, genital organs, wrist, spine. Some were to be fastened to poles in the field, attached to the horns of cattle, tied to the beds of the sick. Color was to bring success in commerce, to prevent disease, to afford safety from shipwreck, lightning, the attack of animals, to assure abundant harvests and favorable control of elements.

Rings, necklaces and bracelets held meaning. They were less associated with opulence and beauty than with use as a practical religious strategy. E.A. Wallis Budge writes, "In the bazaars of Cairo and Tanttah large blue-glazed pottery beads, fully half an inch in diameter, used to be sold to caravan men, who made bandlets of them and tied them to the foreheads of their camels before they set out on their journeys across the desert. The natives believed that the baleful glances of the evil eye would be attracted to the beads, and averted from the animals. . . . It is tolerably certain that the brass bosses and ornaments which decorate the harness of cart horses and shire-stallions were, like the great brass horns which rise from their collars, originally intended to protect the animal from the evil eye; but this fact has been forgotten, and amulets have degenerated into mere ornaments."

In the fashioning of amulets the preferred colors were red, blue, yellow, green, and white. Red stones were efficacious in the treatment of disease and in protecting their wearers from fire and lightning. Blue and violet stones were associated with virtue and faith. They were hung about the necks of children not only to assure the watchfulness of heaven but to make the youngsters obedient to their parents. Yellow stones brought happiness and prosperity. Green stones caused fertility in man and beast and had a mysterious connection with vegetation, rain, and strength generally. White stones averted the evil eye and, because they were thought to come from heaven, carried with them the protection of heaven.

The Romans placed white thorn branches on the doors of their homes, apparently to impale any spirits that attempted to enter. The Russians tied red wool threads around the necks and tails of cattle to drive away witches. In Armenia if a witch was suspected of taking the shape of an animal, the animal was to be shot by putting a silver coin or button in the gun. Norwegians hung white objects in front of their houses to keep the devil out. The Scotch used green branches over homes and barns.

The American Indian used any number of devices and charms. He might paint his body white, then wash himself in a river to cleanse himself of past evils and presumably discourage future ones. Elsewhere in Hungary, Portugal, Denmark, Germany, red strings and bits of red cloth were tied to animals to protect them from death. In Afghanistan, Syria, and Macedonia, blue performed the same magic.

There were also good luck tokens to bless the households of mankind. The Syrians used special red designs. The red hand in Ireland, in India, Constantinople, and Mexico shielded the family from harm. In Jerusalem a blue hand was painted on the doors or walls of dwellings.

The Chinese wrote incantations against demons with red ink on bits of yellow paper. The paper was then burned, its ashes mixed with water, and swallowed. Other talismans consisted of red or yellow strips of paper which were pasted in the home or tied about the neck. One quaint charm was fashioned of bits of colored thread which the Chinese mother assembled from the homes of her neighbors and tied to the dress of her child.

The witches and their cohorts in turn could cast ominous spells. They might stick pins in wax images or other effigies, call upon the Devil to aid them in their nefarious plots.

Heckewelder describes the sad plight of a man being bewitched. "The person thus 'stricken' is immediately seized with an unaccountable terror, his spirits sink, his appetite fails, he is disturbed in his sleep, he pines and wastes away, or a fit of sickness seizes him, and he dies at last a miserable victim to the workings of his own imagination."

Sorcery very much ruled the lives of Australian Aboriginals. Like the Red Ochre Man, the curse of death could also be effected through the practice of "bone pointing." The bone of a bird or animal eaten by an enemy was mixed with grease, red ocher and human hair. A glob of this was stuck to the end of a kangeroo's leg bone and placed near a fire. As the glob melted the person being bewitched would supposedly pass away. Pointing bones have become collector's prizes.

Australian aboriginals had few crafts. Most wore little or no clothing. There were numerous ornaments, beads, rattles, necklaces, charms, a bit of pottery and basket weaving, bark painting, but no textiles made of wool, cotton or flax. Body painting was common and usually was accompanied by elaborate ritual. Pigments were valued and traded among tribes. They might consist of gypsum for white, limonite oxide or the dust from ants' nests for yellow, charcoal for black, ground rock or clay for red ocher. The vehicle to make the pigments usable might be human blood.

What was highly significant in Australia—as well as among primitive peoples everywhere—was that supernatural forces were blamed for all mishaps and disasters. Death itself was considered an unnatural catastrophy, caused by evil forces, human and inhuman, which must be counteracted through complex rites.

Allied to witches, devils and demons were an array of all-powerful gods where favor must be assured through the sacrifice of human life and animals. Christians and Jews are familiar with Biblical sacrifices, many of such being described. Famous is the willingness of Abraham to sacrifice his son, Isaac, whom he had bound and placed upon an altar. But the angel of the Lord appeared and said (Genesis), "Lay not thine hand upon the lad, neither do then anything to him: for now I know that thou fearest God, seeing thou hast not withheld thy son, thine only *son* from me."

Human sacrifice and animal sacrifice have also been associated with color. In ancient Egypt, red-headed youths and red oxen were sacrificed to the gods to assure an abundant harvest. The sacrifice of black animals, like the black cloud, drew rain from the sky, while the sacrifice of white animals brought forth the sun.

In ancient Assyria a priest, clothed in red and smeared with blood, also offered a red-haired and red-cheeked youth to the red planet Mars, and in a temple painted red, with red hangings.

The Romans sacrificed white bulls to Jupiter, as did the Druids to their gods.

According to a Chinese legend of the Tang dynasty, a young girl, chosen by a witch, was married to the Yellow River each year, and then drowned within its waters.

Human sacrifice, mentioned in the Bible, was
commonly practiced in many early civilizations of
Egypt, Assyria, China, Central and South America, to
assuage the gods or seek harmony and security on
earth.

The Japanese sacrificed white boars, white horses, white cocks to appease the gods.

When human sacrifice was practiced among the Aztecs, on the eve of the yearly festival (in July), a young woman portraying the Goddess of the Young Maize was adorned with the upper part of her face red and the lower part yellow. Her legs and arms were covered with red feathers. Her shoes were striped with red. She it was who died for the gods on the summit of the temple, her head chopped off and her heart torn from her breast.

In another Aztec ceremony, a woman, "Our Mother," dressed in white robes, had the upper half of her face painted yellow and the lower half black. Following an elaborate ceremony, her head was chopped off and her heart wrenched out.

In Mexico a sacrificed maiden had her face painted red and yellow in holy token of the colors of the corn.

The Iroquois Indians of America annually sacrificed a white dog to drive away evil and sickness.

From birth to manhood in boys, puberty in girls, to marriage and death, color held essential magic. Caffre boys of Africa were painted white from head to foot at a ceremony of circumcision. Girls at puberty were strangely marked with color. In the Congo the girl's head was shaved and she was smeared with red paint. This and other ceremonies made sure that she would not be barren or give birth to monsters.

In New Guinea the girl at puberty was grotesquely adorned with red stripes on a white ground. In South Australia she was kept in a bower and painted red and white from head to hips. In other parts of Australia she endured a complex ritual. According to Frazer, her mother "decorates her with a waist-band, a forehead-band, and a necklet of pearl-shell, ties green parrot feathers round her arms and wrists and across her chest, and smears her body, back and front, from the waist upwards with blotches of red, white, and yellow paint."

There were similar practices among the Indians of North America. In British Columbia the girl was kept in seclusion and painted red all over, the color being renewed for several days. The Cheyennes of the Missouri valley also used red. If certain rituals were not performed, the girl might poison water, kill fish, destroy crops and bring sickness to anyone she touched.

In the ceremony of marriage, the more sophisticated cultures of the ancient and modern world had charming notions of color and ritual.

Among the ancient Jews the marriage ceremony was performed under the Talis, a golden silk robe supported by four pillars. Around this the bride walked seven times in memory of the siege of Jericho. In India, red paint and even blood were used. Six days before her wedding the Hindu bride wore old tattered yellow garments to drive away evil spirits. Her clothing at the ceremony was yellow, and so, too, were the robes of the priest. And once married, the wife wore yellow upon the return of her husband from a long journey.

In China the bride wore red embroidered with dragons. She was carried in a red marriage chair adorned with lanterns inscribed with the groom's family name in red. She held a red parasol. Red firecrackers were exploded in her behalf. During the rite the bride and bridegroom drank a pledge of wine and honey from two cups which were tied together by a red cord.

In Japan the daughter of a man who fed a thousand white hares in his house would marry a prince. In the Dutch East Indies red or yellow rice was sprinkled over the bridegroom to keep his soul from flying away. Here red was also a love potion, and if the names of boy and girl were written on white paper with the blood of a red hen, the girl would become infatuated when touched by it.

Red and yellow, these were the marriage hues of Egypt, the Orient, Russia, the Balkans—and they still are. In the western countries blue was and is worshipful. An old English rhyme, familiar to everyone, cautions the bride to wear

"Something old and something new.

"Something borrowed and something blue."

Turquoise was the amulet of connubial harmony. It was thought to change color with change of heart and to reconcile man and wife. In Morocco a blue spot was painted behind the bridegroom's ear to thwart the powers of evil. In Ireland the devil himself would curse the newlyweds if some scoundrel attended the ceremony with a red handkerchief tied in knots.

To love, honor, and obey—and to bring forth offspring to populate the earth. In Algeria black hens were sacrificed to promote fertility. In the eastern part of Central Africa the native wife who desired a baby wore blue beads and carried a black hen on her back. In Japan red and white girdles offered protection during pregnancy. Blue and white were so used in France.

Finally, there was much involved ritual associations with death. In China jade was the precious talisman. Its significance is revealed in the burial ceremonies of illustrious and imperial persons. Six jade objects were called upon. With a green tablet, homage was paid to heaven. Yellow paid homage to earth. Green jade respected the region of the east, red jade the region of the south, white jade the region of the west, and black jade the region of the north.

And those who were left to the travails of earth expressed their grief with color. The customs of mourning were and are quite different throughout the world. In China the accepted hue is white. Silks, satins, and red garments are not worn for 27 months after the death of a parent. The hue of visiting cards while in mourning is light brown (the usual color is red). In Japan white is also the emblem of death. When worn in the marriage rite of the Japanese bride, it signifies that she is dead to her family and that she now belongs solely to her husband.

VI

Of Philosopher Stones and Elixirs of Life

According to mystic tradition, the art and science of alchemy originated with the Egyptian Hermes, who, incidentally, was said to father all arts and sciences. It was practiced in Babylonia and Asia Minor and was developed by the Greeks, who passed it on to the Romans and thence to the early Christians.

Later it passed on to Islam where among the Arabs it became a vital science. Today, however, most of the story of Alchemy and the Elixir of Life centers around Europe in the middle ages. Libraries both here and abroad hold magnificent records and illustrated manuscripts devoted to Alchemy. It was, of course, the forerunner of chemistry.

Alchemy is also to be traced to China where it flourished before the Christian era and was involved with the religion of Taoism. The Taoist *Canon,* in fact, is replete with alchemistic writings. The Chinese prepared liquid gold, the Elixir of Life. Jade itself was a solidified liquid that once flowed from a holy mountain. It was to be converted from stone to divine medicine through the magic of a certain herb and used to cure the many ills of mankind.

In Europe, alchemy became the most important of the sciences, all jumbled up with paganism, Christianity, and occultism in general. Among its exponents were men like Roger Bacon, Ben Jonson, Albertus Magnus, Thomas Aquinas, Nicholas Flamel, Raymond Lully, Paracelsus, Jacob Böhme. In the fifteenth century the alchemists banded into a religious and political organization whose initiates penetrated into the sanctuaries of nature, prophesied the future, concealed their formulas in secret writings, doing their best to preserve their necks against the wrath of the church.

While some of these men devoted themselves to the transmutation of metals, all were mystics who saw in alchemy a true expression of their doctrines of human unity. Böhme, for example, was almost wholly transcendental in his theories. To him alchemy was not a physical science at all, but a spiritual one. Thus the Philosopher's Stone as likened unto Christ. Transmutation meant faith, the separation of good from evil, the coarse expunged from the divine.

Of first importance to alchemy were the Seven Metals. The Sun was gold, the Moon silver. Quicksilver was identified with the planet Mercury, iron with Mars, tin with Jupiter, copper with Venus, lead with Saturn. Men believed that the influence of a planet was never stronger than when it acted through its corresponding metal. Also in the various stages of the Work were various regimens each distinguished by colors. These hues appeared as the alchemist busied himself with his furnaces and retorts.

All metals were of one essence, but all were not equally mature. Gold was the highest product and signified regenerate or perfect man. Lead was the basest of metals and signified unregenerate or evil man. Brass, for example, was regarded as being copper on its way to becoming gold. Similarly the whitening of copper by mercury denoted an incomplete transmutation of the substance into silver.

Again, the making of the Philosopher's Stone was said to embody salt, sulphur, mercury, and arsenic—these four being frequently symbolized by a cross. The *prima materia* was the mercury of the philosopher treated with a special sulphur.

The mercury was feminine and composed of water and air. It

Alchemy founded modern chemistry, but it was concerned not merely
with the transmutation of metals, but with spiritual matters. In this old
engraving, Mercury, crowned by cupids, lifts the soul of a man upward
into heaven and leaves his animal body dead on earth.

was positive. Sulphur was masculine and composed of earth and fire. It was negative.

While theories varied, nearly all the alchemists saw the Philosopher's Stone as a divine harmony of the four elements, earth, fire, water, and air. If these could be united the alchemist would have a substance capable of transmuting baser metals into gold and silver and a medicine to cure the diseases of men. One old alchemist wrote, "There abides in nature a certain pure matter, which, being discovered and brought by art to perfection, converts to itself proportionally all imperfect bodies that it touches." The Philosopher's Stone was thus variously described as the harmony of the elements, the crystallization of solar and lunar rays to form virgin earth, a unity of the human with the divine spirit, the Philosopher's Egg (a symbol of creation, enclosing within itself the four elements), and the Spirit of Christ.

Carl Jung in his book *The Integration of the Personality* describes four colors. "The quaternity in alchemy, incidentally, was usually expressed by the four colors of the old painters, mentioned in a fragment of Heraclitus: red, black, yellow, and white; or in diagrams as the four points of the compass. In modern times the unconscious usually chooses red, blue (instead of black), yellow or gold, and green (instead of white). The quaternity is merely another expression of totality. These colors embrace the whole of the rainbow. The alchemists said that the appearance of the *cauda pavonis,* the peacock's tail, was a sign that the process was coming to a successful conclusion."

The process was indeed elaborate—and color was vital to it. John Read, in his *Prelude to Chemistry,* writes: "The various stages necessary for the accomplishment of the Great Work, or preparation of the Philosopher's Stone, was supposed to be marked by the appearance of the characteristic colors: and unless these colors followed one another in proper sequence the operations were dismissed as useless."

The principal hues of alchemy were black, white, gold, and red—and in this specific order. The yellow mentioned by Jung above was omitted as time went on. An old writer states, "The Means or demonstrative signs are Colors, successively and orderly affecting the matter and its affections and demonstrative passions."

Thus black was first and showed the beginning of the action of fire. Its symbol was the cross.

White followed this black and formed perfection of the first degree. Its symbol was the swan.

Third was the color orange or gold, produced in the passage from white to red, a forerunner of the sun, and comparable to the sunrise of dawn.

Fourth was red, symbolized by the phoenix and extracted from white. "The deep redness of the Sun perfecteth the work of Sulphur, which is called the Sperm of the male, the fire of the Stone, the King's Crown, the Son of Sol, wherein the first labor of the workman resteth." Rainbow colors were also to be seen, their fugitive presence having significant meaning and their symbol being the peacock.

To express all this in alchemical formulas, strange emblems of a heraldic nature were used. Sophic sulphur or gold was frequently called the Red King. The White King was sophic mercury or silver. The Ascending Dove or Swan was a white sublimate. The Black Crow was putrefying matter. The Toad was earthly matter. The Winged Lion was mercury. The Wingless Lion was "sulphyr." These devices became a part of writings, useful to impart knowledge to the initiate and a hopeless mystery to the ignorant. Paracelsus wrote: "Soon after your Lili [tincture] shall have become heated in the Philosophic Egg, it becomes, with wonderful appearances, blacker than the crow; afterwards, in succession of time, whiter than the swan; and at last passing through a yellow color, it turns out more red than any blood."

Manly P. Hall in quoting from an old manuscript describes the ten bottles or retorts of the alchemist. References to color are generous. Apparently the original author, like most other alchemists, chose to lend secrecy to his methods in the symbolic language of mysticism. Again, these sacred works of the philosopher were not meant for vulgar mortals. They belonged to the initiate who would understand them and be able to interpret their hidden meanings.

The first bottle, from the mouth of which issued a golden shrub with three blossoms, contained a bluish gray liquid. Under the vessel were the words, "He will have white garments for black then red."

From the mouth of the second bottle issued four golden flowers. This also contained a bluish liquid termed quicksilver.

The third bottle was black, and a golden tree trunk with five cut branches came out of its neck. The substance contained here was described as "Blackness showing through the Head of the Raven."

The fourth bottle was also black, and nothing arose from it. This was the bottle of earth "submerged in Chaos."

The bottom of the fifth bottle contained a bluish gray, spotted liquid. The upper part was filled with a brick-red substance.

The lower half of the sixth bottle was bluish gray, the upper half black. Beside the bottle was a babe: "This newly-born, black son is called Elixir and will be made perfectly white."

The seventh bottle was black at its bottom and black spotted with red above. "Black blacker than black, for many divers colors will appear. Those black clouds will [descend] to the body whence it came, and the junction of body, soul, and spirit has been completed and turned to ashes."

The eighth bottle had a golden band across its center. A golden branch with five leaves reached out from its neck. The substance in the bottle was transparent. "The black clouds are past and the great whiteness has been completed."

A golden white rose came from the neck of the ninth bottle. "He who blanches me makes me red."

Thus the tenth bottle, the consumption of the alchemist's labor, was filled with a blood-red fluid, and from the neck of the vessel sprang a red rose. Now the author says, "I gave to the Master so much silver and gold that he can never be poor."

All this was quite abstruse and more in the esoteric realms than the material. Albertus Magnus was doubtful about the transmutation of metals. Paracelsus declared that alchemy was meant to create elixirs of powerful healing properties. Roger Bacon felt that if the Philosopher's Stone could be formulated and created, it could indeed transmute base metals into gold.

Robert Boyle and Sir Isaac Newton, quite aware of alchemy in their day, while intrigued, were far more concerned with physics than metaphysics.

To pursue the attitude of the great Paracelsus—alchemy for healing—he was one who revolted against the godless attitude of the physicians, those men who treated sickness as a mortal affliction rather than as a divine curse. He declared that the true purpose of alchemy was not to make gold but to prepare efficacious medicines. According to him it was necessary to mix the "rose-colored blood from the Lion," and "the gluten from the Eagle." He believed in the power of the Elixir of Life and manufactured and used it in his cures.

Poor and contaminated blood was the root of all disease. Good blood, the true nostrum, was to be generated by nourishing the sick member with "digested heat." In illness the natural heat of the body was impeded; food was not digested. The heat of the sun and moon must be given the patient. This "heat" was to be extracted from nature by a wonderful and occult art. "Heat acting on moisture generates blackness, and, acting on dryness, generates whiteness, in which redness is hidden."

Further, the spirit of the world and the spirit of the human body were the same. All bodies contained three palpable and visible substances—water, salt, sulphur. "These three things comprise everything created by God, neither more nor less." Water contained nothing beyond the four elements, and so, too, did sulphur. But the salt was special.

In *A Golden and Blessed Casket of Nature's Marvels*, Benedictus Figulus, a disciple of Paracelsus, described how the Elixir of Life was to be made.

First, a glass vessel was used and well sealed so that the spirit of the fluid would not flow out. "For if the Red Spirit escape, the artist labors in vain."

The philosopher proceeded with care. He distilled the liquid with gentle heat.

Later he increased the fire. "Then will rise in the helmet, and distil over, a dry, yellow spirit."

When the helmet was red-hot, the fire was even more increased. "Now the Red Spirit flows out in vapor and the helmet becomes white."

Following this, two elements remained, air and fire, with the impure driven from the pure. "Behold, thou hast now the water in which all metals have their origin, which is of all metals the root! Hence they dissolved in water, even as frozen ice is dissolved into water."

Alchemists of lesser rank were often called puffers. They were chemists at heart but held less fanciful notions than the discovery of miraculous stones and elixirs. De Givry thinks the puffers also deserve credit for the founding of the modern science of chemistry, for much came from their more modest retorts, furnaces and laboratories.

Scientists today seem to have become alchemists again. Oil, water, gas are transmitted into plastics. Diamonds and emeralds are "grown" artificially. Atom bombs have been devised which, in awesome force of destruction, vie with natural forces of earthquake and hurricane. Yet the quest for the Philosopher's Stone must go on, not so much for man's conquest of the world around him, but for control and understanding of the psyche within himself.

VII

Astrology—A Billion Believers

Otherwise intelligent men have been known to sign a manifesto declaring that all of astrology is spurious nonsense. Yet astrology is one of the oldest of "sciences," believed in faithfully by nations, ancient and modern, throughout the world—with millions of "case histories" to support its contentions. Today many Eastern countries still require the wisdom and precognition of astrologers to guide their destinies, to decide upon propitious and hazardous times for state decisions, and otherwise to lead men safely through the uncertainties of life.

Many millions today, in America and western countries, read their horoscopes in the daily newspapers, buy horoscope magazines and paperbacks, perhaps more out of curiosity than for advice, but still motivated by mystic persuasions that have intrigued men since the beginning of time.

Astrology had its beginning in Chaldea four thousand years ago. It had its basis in the music of the spheres, the Sun, Moon, stars, planets and constellations. The planets, which were identified with colors, ruled mankind and were the real powers of

73

the zodiac. The hour of a man's birth might decide his character through the influence of the reigning planet. The affairs of mankind, of kings and slaves, of war, peace, prosperity, want, abundance, and drought were traceable to the movements of the heavenly spheres.

All human beings were born under the influence of the Sun, Moon or planets. Their significance is here described.

The Sun ☉ . The symbolic color was yellow or gold, and the worshipful amulet yellowish—amber, hyacinth, topaz, chrysolite. Born under the rule of the Sun, man acquired fame, riches, honor, and freedom of thought and action. He was wise, shrewd, and eloquent of speech. He was sure to be generous and noble and find favor in the eyes of great men.

The Moon ☽ . The symbolic color was white or silver, and the worshipful amulet whitish—diamond, crystal, opal, beryl, mother-of-pearl. The influence of the Moon produced variety in the affairs of man, causing both success and failure. His domestic relations would be happy. He would be something of a dreamer, religious, compassionate, yet ardent and persevering.

Mars ♂ . The symbolic color was red, and the worshipful amulet reddish—ruby, haematite, jasper, blood-stone. Mars incited a man to deeds of great valor, often amid bloodshed. He was likely to be reckless, to push forward violently toward his ends. Powerful in its influence, Mars often drove from a man all the benign virtues of the other planets.

Mercury ☿ . The symbolic color was neutral, and also the beneficent amulet—agate, carnelian, chalcedony, sardonyx. The influence of Mercury endowed a man with excellent memory. He would be skillful in writing, capable of dealing with life, apt in artistic and scientific work. Yet he might be capricious, deferring to the opinions of others, more attracted to hasty results than to lasting achievements.

Jupiter ♃ . The symbolic color was blue, and the worshipful amulet bluish—amethyst, turquoise, sapphire, jasper, blue diamond. Jupiter made a man honest and blessed him with a deep moral sense. It gave him prudence and suspicion, strength of will, and led him toward ambitions which might as a general rule be successfully but not happily fulfilled.

Venus ♀ . The symbolic color was green, and the worshipful amulet greenish—the emerald and some kinds of sapphire.

Venus influenced a man to love beauty, to be amiable toward men, to have confidence and faith. For all these virtues, however, he might be vain, irresolute, easily tempted, and not very strong to overcome adversity.

Saturn ♄ . The symbolic color was black, the worshipful amulet blackish—jet, onyx, obsidian, diamond, black coral. Saturn created the plodders. Its influence led to introspection, to the contriving of dull and laborious schemes. The man would be learned, trustworthy, diligent, but would have to labor doggedly for his success.

Yet all of astrology was not devoted to the intangible and impalpable mysteries of human fate. The Chinese, for example, were quite practical about the messages they read in the heavens. C.A.S. Williams in his excellent book, *Outline of Chinese Symbolism,* writes, "The appearance of comets, the eclipse of the sun and moon, are believed to have a malign influence over the affairs of men."

There is more as to the planets. The Moon was brooding and melancholy; she was a woman, friendly to the Sun but hostile to Mars. Mercury was the planet of commerce and the arts; he was a man friendly to Jupiter but hostile to Saturn. Venus was the planet of love, a beautiful woman friendly to Mars but hostile to Saturn. The Sun presided over glory and terrestrial riches; he was hostile to Mercury and Saturn. Mars presided over war and battles; he was hostile to the Moon and Mercury, but friendly to Venus. Jupiter was concerned with honors and physical beauty; he was hostile to Mars. Saturn was "the most inauspicious and malefic of all the planets;" he foretold accidents, violent deaths and disasters.

To consider the Chinese again, Mars ruled the summer season. It was the author of punishment and the producer of sudden confusion.

Saturn represented earth, and when it met Jupiter in the same "house" it brought good fortune to the empire. If, however, Saturn with four other planets appeared white and round, mourning and droughts were in store. If the planet was red, disturbances were expected and troops might take the field. If green, there would be floods. If black, sickness and death would descend upon the land. If yellow, China would see a time of prosperity.

Mercury represented water. When white, it forecast the

drought. When yellow, the crops were destined to be scorched. When red, soldiers were expected to attack. When black, floods were imminent. If large and white in the east, the troops beyond the frontier would disperse. If red in the east, the Middle Kingdom would be victorious. Mercury in certain conjunctions with Venus portended many tragedies such as death and the horror of war.

Green clouds in the sky were omens of a plague of locusts. Red clouds meant calamity or warfare. Black clouds brought the floods. Yellow clouds heralded prosperity.

To proceed to the zodiac itself, Manly P. Hall writes, "It is difficult for this age to estimate correctly the profound effect produced upon the religions, philosophies and sciences of antiquity by the study of the planets, luminaries, and constellations."

The word *zodiac* derives from the Greek and means "circle of animals," or "little animals." The name was given to an imaginary zone in the heavens through which the sun, the moon, and the planets traveled. The twelve constellations were twelve "houses" which the sun visited each year.

Each sign of the zodiac thus had its own symbol and color. (The Chinese signs differed from the Greek and consisted of a Rat, Ox, Tiger, Hare, Crocodile, Serpent, Horse, Sheep, Monkey, Hen, Dog, and Pig.) And knowledge of these twelve constellations existed throughout the world, even among the Aztecs of America. In the beginnings of Christianity the Twelve Apostles were associated with the zodiac, as were the twelve tribes of Israel and the twelve gates of heaven mentioned in Revelation. The number is also found in other mythologies and religions.

One of the earliest references to the zodiac is to be found in the Zoroastrian Scriptures of ancient Persia. "Ahura Mazda produced illumination between the sky and the earth, the constellations, then the moon, and afterwards the sun, as I shall relate.

"First he produced the celestial sphere, and the constellation stars are assigned to it by him; especially these twelve whose names are Varak (the Lamb), Tora (the Bull), Dopatkar (the two-figures of Gemini), Kalakang (the Crab), Ser (the Lion), Khusak (Virgo), Tarazuk (the Balance), Gazdum (the Scorpion), Nimasp (the Centaur or Sagittarius), Vahik (Capricornus), Dul (the Waterpot), and Mahik (the Fish); which, from their original creation, were divided into the twenty-eight sub-divisions of the astronomers."

Numerous color designations were given to these signs. First of all they were ruled by the planets.

The Sun which was yellow or gold ruled the sign of Leo the Lion. The Moon was white or silver and ruled the sign of Cancer the crab. Mars was red and ruled the signs of Aries the ram and Scorpio. Mercury was symbolized by a neutral hue and ruled the signs of Gemini the twins, and Virgo the virgin. Jupiter was blue and ruled the signs of Sagittarius the archer and Pisces the fishes. Venus was green and ruled the signs of Taurus the bull and Libra the balance. Saturn, which was black, ruled the signs of Capricorn the goat and Aquarius the water-bearer.

The four elements were also associated with the zodiacal signs: earth with Taurus, Virgo, and Capricorn; water with Cancer, Scorpio, and Pisces; fire with Aries, Leo, and Sagittarius; and air with Gemini, Libra, and Aquarius.

The planets and signs of the zodiac were also, in olden times, related to different parts of the human body. Such associations, however, differed among early astrologers. One famous astrologer, Robert Fludd (1574–1637), Oxford educated London mystic and physician, and advisor to Queen Elizabeth, proposed the following:

Aries the Ram was linked with the head, face, ears and eyes. Taurus the Bull was linked with the neck and gullet, throat and voice. Gemini the Twins was linked with the shoulders and arms. Cancer the Crab was linked with the chest, lungs, ribs and breasts. Leo the Lion was linked with the heart, stomach, diaphragm and back. Virgo the Virgin was linked with the abdomen and intestines. Libra the Balance was linked with the navel, loins, kidneys, buttocks. Scorpio the Scorpion was linked with the sexual organs and bladder. Sagittarius the Archer was linked with the thigh bones. Capricorn the Goat was linked with the knees. Aquarius the Water-Bearer was linked with the lower limbs. Pisces the Fishes was linked with the feet.

Fludd further related the planet Saturn with the brain, Jupiter with the forehead, Mars with the lungs, the Sun with the heart, Venus with the stomach, Mercury the liver, the Moon the intestines. As to the elements, fire inhabited the heart, water the liver, earth the lungs and air the bladder.

This ancient science of astrology, studied enthusiastically to this day, is perhaps not as groundless as the skeptic might suppose. If the stars have nothing to do with a man's destiny, the season of his birth probably does have. The astrologer was a sober man and his work was founded on a careful study of humans—literally millions of them. This experience gave him his clues, his averages. And because of the weight of his "actuarial figures," he probably was more often right than he was wrong.

Today modern scientific investigators tend to confirm much of the astrologer's claim, although the stars may be ignored. Dr. Ellsworth Huntington, for example, has pointed out a possible relationship between the season of a person's birth and the course of his life. It may be that the month of conception holds major significance. Many geniuses, imbeciles, and criminals seem to have birthdays in February, March, and April, the months of conception being May, June, and July. Spring conceptions supposedly follow a definite "urge of nature" among humans as well as lower animals. They naturally result in more impulsive offsprings with extreme personalities. The Hall of Fame gives preference to birthdays in February, March, and April—as well as do most jails! From a record of 3,000 persons suffering from dementia praecox, more of their birthdays were in February and March than in any other months. Who's Who shows a predominance of September and October birthdays, the months of conception being December and January (surely a time when humans are inclined to be more deliberate and therefore "mental" about such matters)!

A January birth seems to influence a person toward the clergy, August toward chemistry. Multiple births occur chiefly in May, June, and July. June and July births are also lowest both in number and "quality."

Records such as these tend to arrive at the same findings of the astrologers. And if skeptics cannot accept the stars, they are at least forced to admit that if persons born in different seasons tend to follow certain life patterns and habits, there is something to learn somewhere.

Because of the fascination of all this there is hardly an adult today who does not have a smattering of the zodiac and whose home does not somewhere contain a paper-bound copy of his horoscope. He still likes to stare into a starry sky, a tyro astrologer naturally curious as to the mysteries of his life.

His sign perhaps is Aries the Ram, ♈ (March 21 to April 19), his color red, his planet Mars. He is ruled by the element fire. He is irascible, vigorous, importunate like the color red itself.

His friend is Taurus the Bull, ♉ (April 20 to May 20), his color a deep green—ruled by Venus and the earth—cold like deep green, slow to anger, courageous.

The Gemini person ♊ (May 21 to June 20) is chestnut brown at heart, ruled by Mercury and air, rich like soil, bountiful with gifts of friendship, strong of heart, prudent, generous— precisely like brown.

The Cancer-born ♋ (June 21 to July 22) is silver like the moon and ruled by water. Like silver and water he reflects the world about him, its joys and sorrows.

Leo ♌ (July 23 to August 22) is golden like the Sun and ruled by fire—self-sufficient, high in aspiration, passionate, eminent.

The child of Virgo ♍ (August 23 to September 21) is controlled by Mercury and earth. His colors are as variegated as he is—glints of yellow wit, blue frankness, red devotion, green sincerity.

The Libra-born ♎ (September 22 to October 21) is ruled by Venus and air. His color is clear green, a friendly and courteous green that blends lucidly with his easy manner and fluent speech.

The child of Scorpio ♏ (October 22 to November 20) is vermilion red, born of Mars and water. He is as imprudent as red, changeable, quick to vengeance and despondency.

Sagittarius the Archer ♐ (November 21 to December 20) is sky-blue, its children ruled by Jupiter and fire—robust, faithful.

Black is the color of Capricorn the Goat ♑ (December 21 to January 19), ruled by Saturn and earth. Its sons are born to shadowy moods of irascibility, triviality, and suspicion.

Gray is the color of Aquarius the Water-Bearer ♒ (January 20 to February 18), ruled by Saturn and air. The child is peaceable like gray, cursed to dwell in gray and moderate circumstances, blessed by a gray temperament. He will know neither white ecstasy nor black despair.

The Pisces born ♓ (February 19 to March 20) is ruled by Jupiter and water. His color is sea-blue—a blue that swells, rises and falls in unending succession, caring not for the experience

There is astrological symbolism here in this 16th century engraving.
Dame Astrology is accompanied by Three Fates, with heaven above and
hell below.

nor profiting from it. . . .

The signs of the zodiac and their symbolic hues pervaded ancient art just as they gave man what he thought to be prescience of his future. They adorned the walls of temples, the coffins of the great, the early churches of Italy, France, and England. The zodiacal amulet, fashioned of its proper gem, was worn on the continents of Africa, Asia, and Europe. One still finds them in the jeweler's shop and on the counters of the syndicate store. Astrology, illusory or not, continues to charm humanity, probably because of an innate sense of wonderment over the enigmas of life.

Astrology in its prime, centuries back, was a branch of occult science, involved with Christianity in Western culture, but not formally either accepted or condemned by the church. It ran contrary also to the doctrine of free will during the period of Enlightenment in the 18th century. Astrologers were respected by pharoahs, emperors, kings, queens, princes and princesses, as well as all mortals of low or high birth.

The old astrologers usually were astronomers as well—or the understudies of astronomers. They looked at the heavens, the stars and planets. Modern astrologers, however, are likely to confine themselves to books and charts. De Givry writes, "So that today we have astrologers—unlikely as it may seem—who never look at the stars, do not even know the stars, never put an eye to a telescope, and would be much embarrassed if asked to point out a single planet or constellation."

VIII

Ancient Nostrums, Talismans, Medics

This chapter also draws heavily from an early book of mine, *The Story of Color,* published some years ago. Around that time I was living in New York, being young, ambitious and capable of demanding work. Over afternoons, evenings, weekends, I polished the seats of wood chairs in general and medical libraries, checked the shelves of second-hand bookstores, bought a collection of new and old volumes and thus assembled a bewildering array of notes which I then tried my best to put in good literary order.

The primitive and the ancient knew little of the workings of the human body. Although they prescribed medicines they were but little practiced in surgery. Flesh and blood consisted of the elements of earth, fire, water, and air. Man sensed, however, that his spirit was animated by some supernatural deity. Man the microcosm absorbed the emanations of god. His body was attuned to the universe. He must preserve this harmony, for disruption brought ruin.

All power was thus with the gods. What of disease? It was an evil spirit that entered the body of man and wrought havoc.

Microbes of course were unknown. In unwary moments the evil one penetrated through the eyes, the ears, mouth, or nose. Death through disease was on every count an assassination!

To effect cures and to preserve health, elaborate ceremonies, invocations, talismans, and colors of divine efficacy were indicated. Plague entered the body like an invisible ghost. It grasped the bones and shook them. It stirred up the fires of fever or immersed the body in an icy sweat. It produced scars and blotches, coated the body with red, yellow, purple, blue, black, gray, or ashen white. Though its marks were apparent, disease itself ever stalked like an apparition.

Countless theories were conceived. Many declared that evil gods and spirits penetrated the human body and threw it into spasms and eruptions. Others saw health as unity, and illness as a disruption of harmony. In Teutonic magic, disease was said to be caused by nine venoms: red, white, purple, yellow, green, livid, blue, brown, and crimson. These were banished from the human system by special ceremonies known to the elect. "Then took Wodan nine magic twigs, smote then that serpent that in nine bits she flew apart. Now these nine herbs avail against nine spirits of evil, against nine venoms and against nine winged onsets."

The use of herbs was one of the earliest of remedies. Many of these brought actual physical benefit and were perhaps discovered through trial and error methods. Yet in many cases the magic was based on weird associations only. Almost any substance might be used—fungus from a grave, dew from grass, noxious concoctions that were often little more than fantastic inventions. Again, the healer would associate the form of a plant with the affliction itself. The juices of fern and moss were good for the hair. The *Palma Christi,* shaped like a hand, cured the hand. Another plant, tooth-shaped, relieved the ache of a tooth. The onion, with its rings and layers, was thought to possess healing virtues because it was supposed to be designed like the world itself. The strong odor of garlic was thought to exude powers that chased away illness. There were healing stones that drove men mad, stopped the barking of dogs, expelled demons, or turned black in the hands of false witnesses.

Most of the symbolism of color in healing was quite direct. Colors were associated with disease because disease produced color. Plants, flowers, minerals, elixirs were efficacious when their hues resembled the pallor of the flesh or the sores upon it. Thus, red, yellow, and black had great medicinal value, for they were identified respectively with fever, plague, and death.

Red is the most interesting of all colors in magic healing. It is found not only in the lore of ancient medicine but in the superstitions of modern times. Scarlet cloth has for many centuries been used to stop bleeding. Avicenna in the eleventh century dressed and covered his patients with red. The physician to Edward II, to thwart smallpox, directed that everything about the room be red. Francis I was treated in a scarlet blanket for the same affliction. The children of one of the Mikados were surrounded by red in all furnishings during an attack of the disease.

At times the physician would go to the extremes of prescribing red medicines and foods so that everything the patient ate or saw was crimson. The custom was so persistent that English physicians once wore scarlet cloaks as a distinguishing mark of their profession. In the rural districts of Massachusetts, before the days of telephones, a red flag was once displayed to call the doctor as he made his rounds.

In Ireland and Russia red flannel was a remedy for scarlet fever. The Russians, indeed, held great faith in the color red. If a skein of red wool was wound around the arms and legs, it would ward off agues and fever. Nine skeins wound around a child's neck would prevent scarlet fever.

On the Greek island of Karpathos, the priest tied a red thread around the neck of a sick person. The next day friends could remove the thread, tie it around a tree and thus transfer the illness to the tree.

Red wool cured sprains in Scotland, sore throat in Ireland, and prevented fevers in Macedonia. Red thread was thought necessary in the teething of English children.

The breath of a red ox was a palliative in convulsions. Red sealing wax cured certain eruptions. Red coral kept teeth from loosening in England and relieved headaches in Portugal. Red overcame nightmares in Japan. In Macedonia red yarn was tied on the bedroom door after the birth of a child to bind evil.

Erysipelas, called St. Anthony's fire, being red, could be relieved if a person carried a stick of red sealing wax or a piece of blood-stone. In Bavaria, Saxony, Bohemia, peasants' cottages had red birds (crossbills) in cages to draw St. Anthony's fire from the afflicted. And, as an extra benefit, fire and lightning would not strike the cottage.

In China the ruby was worn to promote long life. A ribbon of red cloth was tied to the pigtail of the child for the same reason. The garnet in India and Persia similarly protected their wearers. Roman coral and red carnelian drove away the evils of disease.

Budge has written of those red amulets which were common also in Egypt centuries ago: "A considerable number of rings made of red jasper, red *faïence,* and red glass have been found in the tombs of Egypt; all are uninscribed and all have a gap in them. How and why they were used is not known, but a recent view about them is that they were worn as amulets by soldiers and by men whose work or duties brought them into conflict with their enemies, to prevent them from being wounded, or if wounded, to stop the flow of blood. It is possible that they were worn by women to prevent bleeding."

Yellow cured jaundice because jaundice was yellow. In Germany the disease was attacked with yellow turnips, gold coins, saffron, and a dozen other yellowish things. Yellow spiders rolled in butter were English remedies. In one part of Russia gold beads were worn. In another section the patient gazed at a black surface, this being the opposite of yellow and therefore capable of drawing the jaundice from the system. In India jaundice was banished to yellow bodies, creatures, and things such as the sun, where it properly belonged. The red, vigorous color of health was then "drawn" from a bull after certain recitations by a priest. An old text states, "Up to the sun shall go thy heart-ache and thy jaundice: in the color of the red bull do we envelop thee. We envelope thee in red tints, unto long life. May this person go unscathed and be free of the yellow color!"

In Greece an affliction called "gold disease" was cured when the patient drank wine in which a gold piece had been placed and exposed to the stars for three nights. Bits of gold were also sprinkled on food as a safeguard against poisoning.

Plutarch wrote that if a person suffering from jaundice stared at the yellow eye of a bird (which had a yellow eye) the disease could be cured. He wrote, "Such is the nature, and such is the temperament of the creature that it draws out and receives the malady which issues, like a stream, through the eyesight."

In one of the Malay states disease and plague were driven away in a yellow ship—or a buffalo covered with red pigment lumbered out of the village with the scourge upon him.

Among the ancient Greeks it was thought that the eggs of a raven would restore blackness to the hair. So effective was the remedy thought to be that the Greek kept his mouth filled with oil while the egg was rubbed into his hair in order to keep his teeth from turning black. Black threads from the wool of black sheep cured earache in Ireland, England and parts of Vermont. Black snails were rubbed on warts.

In France the skins of black animals, applied while warm to the limbs of the body, relieved rheumatism. Black fowl if buried where caught would cure epilepsy. The blood of a black cat has been prescribed for pneumonia in places as remote from each other as England and South Africa.

Plutarch mentions that a white reed found on the banks of a river while one journeyed to sacrifice at dawn, if strewn in a wife's bedroom, drove an adulterer mad and forced him to confess his sin. The milk of a white hare cured fever in Brittany.

Few other colors are found in amulets and charms meant to cure disease. Blue and green have mostly been used as preventives, to ward off the evil eye, and to spare the wearer from the visitation of demons. However, in Ireland blue ribbon was used for the croup, and indigestion was relieved when a person measured his waist with a green thread in the name of the Trinity and then ate three dandelion leaves on a piece of bread and butter for three consecutive mornings.

Because disease came mysteriously out of nature, the most potent hues to combat it must also come out of nature. Thus precious and semi-precious stones were particularly therapeutic.

Brown agate drove away fevers, epilepsy, madness. It stopped the flow of rheum in the eye, reduced menstruation, dispersed the water of dropsy.

Amber was mixed with honey for earache or failure of sight. Amber dust relieved pains in the stomach and helped the kidneys, liver and intestines. The smell of burnt amber aided women in labor. An amber ball, held in the palm of the hand, reduced fever and even kept a man cool on the hottest of days. Amber beads preserved the wearer from rheumatism, toothache, headache, rickets, jaundice. A bit placed in the nose stopped bleeding. About the neck it made the largest goiter disappear.

The Arab physician used powdered amber to prevent miscarriage, to overcome boils, carbuncles, ulcers.

Amethyst cured the gout. Placed under the pillow it gave the sleeper pleasant dreams.

Asphalt, or bitumen, preserved a man from sprains, fracture of the bones, blows, headaches, epilepsy, dizziness, and palpitation of the heart.

Green beryl, through sympathetic magic, overcame diseases of the eye. Yellowish beryl was prescribed for jaundice and a bad liver.

Carnelian, the "blood stone," restrained the hemorrhage and removed blotches, pimples, and sores from the flesh.

According to Budge the cat's eye was washed in milk and the liquid drunk by the Sudanese Kordofan's wife. Should she commit adultery after his departure no child would be born of the illicit union.

Chalcedony lowered fever and eased the passage of gall stones.

Crystal was used as a burning-glass in medical operations. In powder form it was a cure for swellings of the glands, diseased eyes, heart disease, fever, and intestinal pains. Mixed with honey it increased the milk of a mother.

Coral overcame sterility.

The diamond fortified mind and body. It cured practically everything. Dipped in water and wine it created an elixir that thwarted gout, jaundice, and apoplexy.

The emerald cured disease of the eyes.

The garnet prevented skin eruptions.

Haematite cleared blood-shot eyes, stopped hemorrhages of the lungs and uterus, prevented sunstroke and headaches.

Jade assisted in childbirth. It cured dropsy, quenched the thirst, relieved palpitation of the heart.

Jasper was helpful in pregnancy.

Jet healed epilepsy, toothache, headache, glandular swellings.

Lapis Lazuli prevented miscarriage.

Opal cured diseases of the eye.

Peridot was a palliative for various diseases of the liver.

The ruby was dipped in water for a stomachic and ground into powder to check the flux of blood.

Sapphire prevented disease and plague.

Turquoise protected its wearer from poison, the bites of

reptiles, diseases of the eye. Dipped or washed in water it charged the liquid and made it a palliative for those who suffered from the retention of urine.

Men today are taught to be wary of nostrums. One must not forget, however, that amulets, charms, and colors were once recognized, used, and endorsed by the foremost medical practitioners of ancient times.

Perhaps there are universal laws of harmony which gave efficacy to charms and colors ages ago. At least man still has the instinct to believe in magic, to look upon science as cold-blooded and agnostic.

The modern physician traces the art of medicine to Hippocrates; the occultist goes back still farther and bows at the shrine of Hermes the great.

Hermes, the Thrice Greatest, Master of All Arts and Sciences, Perfect in All Crafts, Ruler of the Three Worlds, Scribe of the Gods, and Keeper of the Books of Life, is perhaps the most remarkable figure in the history of mysticism. Accepted both as a god and a mortal in Egypt, he was revered by the Greeks and became the Mercury of the Romans. He is said to have been the author of twenty thousand or more books, these works founding the entire mythology of the ancient world and dealing with medicine, alchemy, law, art, astrology, music, magic, philosophy, mathematics, and anatomy. Francis Barrett thus finds reason to say of him, "If God ever appeared in man, he appeared in him."

The famous Emerald Tablet, said to have been found in the valley of Ebron, epitomizes the teachings of the amazing Hermes. It contains an alchemical formula and involves color simply because color is part of alchemy and in turn obedient to one supreme and divine entity associated with light. Did Hermes heal with color? Unquestionably he did, for the Egypt that was his abounds in many symbols. One ancient papyrus exclaims, "Come verdigris ointment! Come thou verdant one!"

The Egyptians believed in the efficacy of the spectrum, the power of charms, gems, and hues. In one papyrus dating back nearly four thousand years the age-old problem of revealing the sex of an unborn child was answered in these words: "Another time: if thou seest her face green . . . she will bring forth a male child, but if thou seest things upon her eyes, she will not bear ever." Again, in the Zoroastrian Scriptures, reference is made to

Hermes, the Thrice Greatest, Master of All Arts and Sciences. He was supreme both as a god and mortal to the Egyptians, was revered by the Greeks and became Mercury to the Romans. He wrote twenty thousand books and founded all arts, philosophies and sciences.

the causes of sex in the unborn: "The female seed is cold and moist, and its flow is from the loins, and the color is white, red, and yellow; and the male seed is hot and dry, its flow is from the brain of the head, and the color is white and mud-colored."

In Asia Minor the ancient Persians understood and practiced a sort of color therapy based on the emanations of light. The Babylonians believed that the seat of all passions and emotions was in the liver, not in the heart. When the sun god created man, he arranged his entrails in such a way that they would indicate the will of the deity. Thus the liver was studied and even employed in sacrificial rites and ceremonies (using sheep).

Numerous Egyptian surgical and medical manuscripts have been found. One of the most fascinating of these is the Papyrus Ebers dating back to about 1500 B.C. and said to be "the oldest [complete] book the world possesses."

The manuscript is beautifully preserved and wholly intact throughout its 110 wide columns and 68-foot length. It consists of a collection of the medical prescriptions. "Throughout the manuscript the heading of the different chapters, the names of the diseases, the directions for treatment, and in many cases the weights and dosages of the drugs are written in vivid red."

Here one finds undoubtedly the first advice to apply raw meat to a black eye!

Colored minerals, malachite, red and yellow ochre, and haematite (a red clay) are endowed with efficacy apparently because of their hue.

For constipation—white or red cake.

To salve a wound—vermilion writing fluid mixed with goat's fat and honey.

For other ailments—the blood of a black cat and numerous other colored things, organic and inorganic.

In Greece the Egyptian theories prevailed. White garments were worn by the afflicted to cause pleasant dreams. Pythagoras, like Hermes, also taught of unity and harmony. To him god was a living and absolute truth clothed in light. He was acquainted with the Mysteries and declared the motion of god to be circular, his body composed of the substance of light. Everything in nature was divisible into three parts. There was the supreme and spiritual world, the home of the deity. There was the superior world, the home of the immortals. And there was the inferior world, the home of mankind.

Although the exact practices of Pythagoras are unknown, he is said to have cured disease through the aid of music, of poetry, and color.

Unlike Pythagoras, whose credo was one of universal harmony, the great Hippocrates (460?–377? B.C.) cast suspicious eyes on the habits of men, talked about their diets, listened to the beating of their hearts and founded that critical and diagnostic attitude which is a part of modern medicine. Here perhaps came the beginning of a new viewpoint—color as an outward expression of an internal and strictly pathological condition. And Hippocrates, too, prognosticated the sex of the unborn in terms of color: "A woman with child, if it be a male, has a good color, and if a female, she has a bad color."

Celsus (A.D. 14?), who lived at the beginning of the Christian era, followed the doctrines set forth by Hippocrates. His attitude toward color was also practical rather than occult, although superstition did influence him at times. For example, he prescribed medicines with color in mind—white violets, purple violets, the lily, iris, narcissus, rose, saffron. The plasters he used to relieve wounds were black, green, red, and white. Of red he wrote, "There is one plaster almost of a red color, which seems to bring wounds very rapidly to cicatrize."

Celsus declared spring to be the most salubrious season, then winter and summer, with autumn most inimical. Regarding the insane, he wrote, "It is best . . . to keep him in light who dreads darkness; and to keep him in darkness who dreads light." One of his potions was yellow: "Saffron ointment with iris-oil applied on the head, aids in procuring sleep, and also in tranquilizing the mind."

Galen (130–200 A.D.) said, "I have been anointed with the white ointment of the tree of life," and thereby was the mystic. He was attracted to motion and change as significant in diagnosis. "Thus, if that which is white becomes black, or that which is black becomes white, it undergoes motion in respect to *color.*" He worked out an elaborate theory in which these visible changes were reckoned with. One of his queries in this connection is amusing. "How, then, could blood ever turn into bone without having first become, as far as possible, thickened and white? And how could bread turn into blood without having gradually parted with its whiteness and gradually acquired redness?"

During the Dark Ages progress in medicine passed from Rome to Islam and found its greatest leader in Avicenna, an Arabian (980–1037?). In his *Canon of Medicine,* one of the most venerable of medical documents, he pays rare tribute to color both as a guide in diagnosis and as an actual curative. Avicenna's attitude was more searching and passionate than that of Hippocrates, Celsus, or Galen. Color was of vital importance, worthy of profound study. In consequence the Arabian dealt freely with it and wrote it into almost every page of his *Canon.*

Avicenna was an acknowledged disciple of Aristotle. The world to him comprised five elements which he allied to the senses, the mind, and the emotions. These elements—earth, water, fire, air, ether—created tendencies which formed the body and soul of man. Also, a man's breathing had different phases, strong and weak, and the vibration rates of breath were related to the elements. The breath of earth was slow, the breath of ether fine and quick.

As to the elements, earth was related to the bones and skeleton of man, to his sense of touch, to mental torpor, obstinacy and fear. Water was related to the muscles, to the sense of taste, to that which was lymphatic, submissive, affectionate. Fire was related to the liver and blood, to the sense of smell, to optimism, anger, vexation. Air was related to the vascular and cutaneous system, to the sense of hearing, to cheerfulness and humor. Ether was related to the nervous system and hair, to the sense of vision, to temperaments that were reflective and sad.

Avicenna diagnosed the diseases of his patients with an eye on hue. The color of hair and skin, of eyes, of excrement and urine were significant. "In jaundice, if the urine becomes of a deeper red until it is nearly black, and if its stain on linen can no longer be removed, it is a good sign—the better the deeper red. But if the urine becomes white or slightly reddish, and the jaundice is not subsiding, the advent of dropsy is to be feared."

If the skin of the patient changed to yellow, he suspected a disorder of the liver. If the change was to white, the disorder was probably in the spleen. A yellowish green complexion might be attributed to piles. All these hues must be carefully observed.

Avicenna devoted much study to the fluids and humors of the body. He developed an unusual chart in which color was related to temperament and to the physical condition of the body.

These conclusions he based on experience, and he made use of them in his practice.

The predecessors of the great Arabian had also noted that color was an observable symptom in disease. But Avicenna was more of a mystic. Color was not only the sign of affliction—it might also be the cure! First of all, the innate temperaments of men might be found written in the color of their hair. People with black hair had hot temperament of the tawny-headed or red-headed person was equable. Here there was an excess of "unburnt heat"; hence there was proneness to anger. The temperament of the fair-haired was cold and very moist; that of the gray-headed was cold and very dry. In both these instances Avicenna saw weakness and physical degeneracy. Men, like plants, lost color when they dried!

Of humors he wrote: "Even imagination, emotional states and other agents cause the humors to move. Thus, if one were to gaze intently at something red, one would cause the sanguineous humor to move. This is why one must not let a person suffering from nose-bleeding see things of a brilliant red color." He also declared red and yellow to be injurious to the eye. Blue light soothed the movement of the blood; red light stimulated it. The clear light of morning aided nutrition.

Avicenna thus had every confidence in the therapy of color. Because red moved the blood this hue was used profusely and even prescribed in medicines. White, conversely, was a refrigerant. Potions of red flowers cured disorders of the blood. Yellow flowers cured disorders of the biliary system.

Brilliant Avicenna! With Paracelsus, of kindred spirit, he was to be excommunicated by the medical profession, his red, white, and yellow flowers set aside for chemicals, antibiotics, microscopes and syringes.

The real name of Paracelsus was Theophrastus Bombastus von Hohenheim (1493–1541). Although born of the Renaissance, his spirit was nourished by the involved teachings of the alchemist and the superstition of the medieval friar.

To Paracelsus, man had a five-fold being. First was his visible form, his physical body. Second was his etheric body, identified with his glandular system. Third was his astral body, whose organ was the nervous system. Fourth was his ego, which found expression through the blood vessels. And fifth was his Higher Self.

He also related the body of man to the seven ruling planets. The Sun ruled the heart, the Moon the brain, Saturn the spleen, Mercury the lungs, Venus the kidneys, Jupiter the liver, and Mars the gall.

Paracelsus was as bombastic as his name. On one occasion, preceding a series of lectures at Basel, he publicly burned the works of Galen and Avicenna, thereby showing his contempt for past and contemporary medicine. Disease was caused by inharmony. The body of man was a compound of salt, sulphur, and mercury, and the separation of these elements (which were of a mystic nature) produced illness. All "relaxing" diseases such as dysentery and diarrhea were generated from salt. Diseases of the heart and brain arose from sulphur. Diseases of the ligaments, bones, arteries, and nerves arose from the element mercury.

He was an alchemist at heart and believed in the efficacy of elixirs. Color and light were vital. He wrote: "Whatever tinges with a white color has the nature of life, and the properties and power of light, which produces life. Whatever, on the other hand, tinges with blackness, or produces black, has a nature in common with death, the properties of darkness, and forces productive of death."

Paracelsus healed with invocations, with the divine vibrations of music and color, with talismans and charms, with herbs and the regulation of diet, and through bleeding and purging. These cures of his were at times miraculous, and his genius was known throughout Europe.

Today the occultist believes that Paracelsus is still one of the great healers of all times. However, his theories failed to have lasting influence on the progress of medicine. After him came Vesalius the anatomist, Leewenhoek and his microscope, then men like Pasteur and Koch. Disease was caused by the attack of an army of microbes. To argue about the harmony of natural and supernatural forces seemed irrelevant in view of the evidence of squirming germs.

Thus, following Paracelsus, the therapy of color was abandoned for over two hundred years. Men were to try their skill at alchemy, at the concoction of the Philosopher's Stone, the Elixir of Life. Despite all, color was to be a nostrum right up to modern times, revived with considerable glory in the nineteenth century by men like Edwin D. Babbitt, presumably slain in the beginning of the twentieth century and then accepted again, cautiously, by men of science, psychologists and psychiatrists, who have not lost sight of the fact that man is heir to psychic disturbances just as well as to physical ones, and that mind and body are much in sympathy with each other.

IX

The Shaman and the Witch Doctor

The shaman, the witch doctor, the medicine man were sorcerers for the most part, practicing magic and relying on no end of devices to drive away evil and cure sickness. While the term shaman traces back to Siberian tribes in Russia, the witch doctor and the medicine man are best associated with the American Indian.

Let it be understood that, even today, far more human beings consult shamans than they do the graduates of medical colleges! And the shaman, without question, does cure a lot of his superstitious patients. Not alone this, but he often was called upon to foretell the future, bring rain, drive away evil spirits, and expose thieves and murderers. If he were angry, he might also cast spells and bring bad luck. However, if he were a privileged man, his profession had its risks; the death of too many patients might bring death to himself.

Shamanism is best identified with primitive peoples in North and South America, among Eskimos, Lapps and tribes in the Far East. The world was thought to be visited by good and evil spirits. These spirits could incarnate themselves and take possession

THE MAGICIAN.

of the unsuspecting, upon which tragedy would strike.

Maybe this all goes back to the hunting culture of prehistoric times when men covered themselves with animal furs, attached horns to their heads and set forth to stalk food. As has been noted in the chapter on sorcery, animal-slayers (and manslayers) needed to protect themselves from the furious souls of the annihilated. Thus from hunting, to protection from demons, to the curing of disease, the primitive hunter logically became the witch doctor and medicine man.

Shamans functioned as healers, priests, soothsayers, exorcisers and leaders, and were distinguished indeed. Their magic involved incantations, herbs, remedies, nostrums, amulets. They might go into a trance, dance, tremble, have convulsions, pass out, have dreams and hallucinations and otherwise engage in tantrums not normally indulged in by average persons.

More allied to medicine, they might engage in bloodletting, pounding, kneading, hypnotism. They were familiar with curative drugs, such as quinine, and narcotics such as peyote. They might fast and give themselves to self-torture. They had secret rites, magic words to recite, magic gestures to reveal.

They could claim divine powers, hold direct contact with the spirit world. They could transport themselves into realms beyond the earth, wander into lands unknown to ordinary mortals.

Their equipment: headdress, garments, furs, antlers, masks, necklets, belts, leggings, boots, jewelry and charms, drums, beads, rattles, staffs, wands—and colors.

Commonly they dressed as animals or birds: bear, stag, beaver, otter, lion, tiger, eagle, hawk. They could be the sun and the moon. They dealt with human lives and souls, and had the blessings of the gods.

Anthropologists have studied the mythology, mysticism and rituals of primitive peoples throughout the world. Descriptive monographs exist by the hundreds, but are difficult to find and locate. Two excellent sources consulted by this writer are *The Golden Bough* by Sir James George Frazer in 12 volumes, and *The Mythology of All Races* edited by Canon John Arnott McCulloch in 10 volumes. (These were also referred to for the chapter on Sorcery.)

Among the most *bewitching* medicine men of the world are those of the American Indian. Their traditions and ceremonies have been well studied and reported. In the eastern parts of North America, as witnessed in the late 18th and early 19th centuries, magic healing, witchcraft, and sorcery were prevalent among the tribes. The Indian witch doctor apparently was well admired and conducted a lucrative practice in tangible goods and wampum. Rev. John Heckenwelder has related, "If the patient who applies, is rich, the *Doctor* will never fail, whatever the complaint may be, to ascribe it to the powers of witchcraft, and recommend himself as the only person capable of giving relief in such a hard and complicated case. The poor patient, therefore, if he will have the benefit of the great man's advice and assistance, must immediately give him his *honorarium,* which is commonly either a fine horse, or a good rifle-gun, a considerable quantity of wampum, or goods to a handsome amount. When this fee is well secured, and not before, the Doctor prepares for the hard task that he has undertaken with as much apparent labour as if he was about to remove a mountain."

What caused illness? Mostly it was the evil work of demons who must be cast out from the afflicted one. While there might be some definite therapy in herbs, the bark of trees, roots, flowers and the like, the most impressive magic, visually, was in the ritual and dress of the doctor. He was supposed to have supernatural powers and be able to call upon divine and potent sources. Maybe the sick man had been cursed by a witch. Maybe his soul had left his body. Whatever, the medicine man would proceed to set everything back in natural order.

Standing before his patient he puts on a grave aspect, accompanied by weird contortions, gestures and "antic tricks." He breaths on the patient, blows into his mouth, squirts potions onto his face, mouth, nose. He rattles a gourd filled with dry beans or pebbles, produces a number of sticks and bundles, making a clatter which presumably would frighten the evil spirit of the patient away. Finally exhausted, he departs, only to return from time to time to see if his patient has recovered or if he has passed away.

If the medicine man fails, he may claim that the patient was incurable, that the doctor had not been called in time, or that his prescriptions had not been followed. However, if the doctor loses too many patients, his own life might be in jeopardy.

Color entered into the dress of the medicine man.

This painting by George Catlin has the title "Medicine Man Performing His Mysteries Over a Dying Man." Catlin's studies of American Indians and Indian life during the middle of the 19th century were made through personal observations. His Medicine Man is undoubtedly authentically dressed. (National Collection of Fine Arts, Smithsonian Institution, gift of Mrs. Sarah Harrison.)

Heckenwelder offers this description. "The jugglers' dress, when in the exercise of their functions, exhibits a most frightful sight. I had no idea of the importance of these men, until by accident I met with one, habited in his full costume. As I was once walking through the street of a large Indian village on the Muskingum, with the chief *Gelelemend,* whom we call *Kill-buck,* one of those monsters suddenly came out of the house next to me, at whose sight I was so frightened, that I flew immediately to the other side of the chief, who observing my agitation and the quick strides I made, asked me what was the matter, and what I thought it was that I saw before me. 'By its outward appearance,' answered I, 'I would think it a bear, or some such ferocious animal, what is *inside* I do not know, but rather judge it to be the *Evil Spirit.*' My friend Kill-buck smiled, and replied, 'O! no, no; don't believe that! it is a man you well know, it is our *Doctor.*' 'A Doctor!' said I. 'What! a human being to transform himself so as to be taken for a bear walking on his hind legs, and with horns on his head? You will not, surely, deceive me; if it is not a bear, it must be some other ferocious animal that I have never seen before.' "

Among western and southwestern American Indian tribes, even greater sophistication might be shown. Most of my readers will recall pictures of the elaborate dress, colors, rituals of Navajo, Creek, Pueblo and other Indians. The Navajos made paints in white, red, yellow, blue, black. William Z. Park writes, "The use of two native paints, red and white, is very common in curing practices. Both of these paints are secured from natural deposits of earth. The uses to which the paints are used are manifold: the bodies and faces of both shamans and spectators are painted, the patient is sprinkled with the dry powder, and the feathers and the wand used in curing are painted." Some Navajo medicine men were skilled artists. Some made beautifully designed sand paintings as part of healing ritual, and these might of necessity be destroyed before the sun went down.

Among the Blackfoot, the medicine man might paint a youth yellow to give him the power of the sun. The aching joints of those in pain might be painted red. The Creek doctor had gourds, rattles, drums, knives, beads. When he treated gunshot wounds he wore a buzzard's feather. For snake bites he donned fox skin and carried a pouch of opossum skin. He painted black circles around his eyes as a mark of identification. He sang, chanted, danced.

He could charm animals as well as men.

There is a "peyote cult" among the Indians of the Rio Grande Valley. The taking of peyote has effects similar to those of LSD described in a later chapter It stimulates religious ecstasy, causes hallucinations, heightens sensitivity to color and holds great spiritual meaning for some tribes.

Heinrich Klüver's book on *Mescal and Mechanism of Hallucinations* describes a peyote ceremony conducted by Tarahumare Indians under the guidance of a shaman. There is a preliminary journey and pilgrimage to peyote territory where the drug is harvested from cactus. Men are specially chosen for this expedition. They fast for several days, are purified by the burning of copal incense, and they erect crosses where the rare plants are found. The peyote is then gathered by prescribed ritual and some of it eaten. After its effects are worn off, the Indians return home where they are welcomed with song and a sacrificial feast. Klüver quotes Schonle in describing the ceremony. Women appointed by the shaman grind the peyote, wash it and produce a brown liquid.

"When evening comes, the shaman seats himself west of the fire with a male assistant on either side and the women assistants to the north of the fire. A cross is placed to the east of the fire. On a symbol of the world a peyote plant is placed and covered with a hollow gourd which is used by the shaman as a resonator for his rasping stick.

"The order of the ceremony consists of singing by the shaman to the accompaniment of the rasping which continues through the night; offering of incense to the cross by assistants who kneel and cross themselves; dancing by the male assistants who wear white blankets and carry rattles of deer-hoofs (this dance follows a line contrary to the motion of the sun and occupies the space between the fire and the cross with a later extension to include the fire); dancing by the women assistants; drinking of the peyote by all who are in attendance. The only variation in the procedure comes at daybreak when the people gather near the cross for the healing service. This is accomplished not by the direct use of the peyote, which is, nevertheless, thought to have curative power, but by rasping against the person's head, the slight dust from the rasping being thought efficacious in producing health. After healing the people, the shaman rasps toward the rising sun to waft the peyote spirit home. The ceremony ends with this service and is followed by a feast."

X

Edwin D. Babbitt—Miracle Man

In 1878 one of the most fascinating of books in the literature of color was published in New York: *The Principles of Light and Color,* by Edwin D. Babbitt. It was devoted to "The Harmonic Laws of the Universe, the Etherio-Atomic Philosophy, Chromo Therapeutics, and the General Philosophy of Fine Forces, together with Numerous Discoveries and Practical Applications." This made Babbitt a mystic, scientist and healer all at the same time.

Babbitt's work had been known to me during my youth. A first edition of his book, rare at the time, cost me $50.00 (It is worth far more today.) Babbitt fathered numerous disciples and avatars, many cults of chromotherapy which still exist today, not alone in America but in England and Australia. He has been quoted and plagiarized time and again. My collection of books on the occult aspects of color number about two dozen that owe their inspiration to Babbitt. I have corresponded with "color healers" here and abroad for several decades.

In 1967, University Books asked me to edit Babbitt's master-

work. To this I happily agreed, only to be accused on one occasion of lowering my professional integrity by reviewing the nonsense of a charlatan. To my own defense, however, I emphasized that, fakir or miracle healer (I wouldn't take sides), Babbitt was a genius in his day, a tremendous influence in the age-old and engaging mysteries of color therapy, and his *Principles* were well worthy of summary and perpetuity.

Edwin D. Babbitt was born in Hamden, New York, on February 1, 1828, the son of a Congregational minister. He was well educated and traveled widely in America and abroad. He married in 1857 and had five children, one of whom became the eminent humanist philosopher at Harvard, Irving Babbitt.

Edwin began as a teacher, then wrote and published a series of copy books known as Babbittonian Penmanship which were issued in New York and London. He sold pens, inks and pencils to the school field.

Apparently around the age of 40, Babbitt, religious by training and nature, took an interest in things metaphysical, becoming a "magnetist" and "psychophysician." New York City directories referred to him in terms of "penmanship," "stationer," "publisher," "importer." Then in 1875–76 the directory announced "magnetist and author of health guide."

Babbitt created a brilliant world with much of its basis in color. His *Principles of Light and Color,* published in 1878, had astounding impact and established him as one of the miracle men of his day—and for many decades to follow. Bear in mind that these were days of patent medicines, snake oil, magnetic belts. Simply through desire, a man could call himself a doctor and treat patients at will. His work was variously praised and condemned. Babbitt's "fine forces," his "harmonic laws of the universe," were difficult for many to accept. From 1888 to 1894 he headed The New York College of Magnetics and presumably treated numerous human ailments with color. He died in 1905 at the age of 77. "Chromopathy is based on eternal truth, and the sooner any great truth is adopted, the better it is for all concerned."

Before Babbitt, however, there had been two Philadelphians who had experimented with color and written unique books—and both were duly acknowledged in Babbitt's *Principles.*

The first was A. J. Pleasanton, whose *Blue and Sun-Lights*

appeared in 1876. To him, the blue sky held the secret of the bounty of life. Blue "for one of its functions, deoxygenates carbonic acid gas, supplying carbon to vegetation and nurturing both vegetable and animal life with its oxygen."

He constructed a special greenhouse which had one pane of blue glass for every eight panes of clear. Working with grapes he claimed to develop more abundant fruit. The plants were free of maladies, and even insects and flies were driven away by the magic of blue. (Today, the Dutch are said to paint the interiors of cattle barns blue to repel flies.)

Pleasanton also experimented with pigs and endeavored to prove that blue light tended to increase their weight.

The second man, S. Pancoast, published his *Blue and Red Light* in 1877. What later irritated the rational scientist is that he wrote in mystic terms. "Our reader has, we trust, learned to respect, as we do, the Ancient Sages, at whom modern Scientists, in their overweening self-esteem, their ignorant vainglory, are wont to scoff."

Pancoast believed that "White is the color of the Quintescence of Light; toward its negative pole, White is condensed in Blue, and fixed in Black; toward its positive pole, White is condensed in Yellow, and fixed in Red. Blue invites to repose, or to slumber, Black is absolute rest, the sleep of death; Yellow is activity, Red is absolute motion, the motion of life; and White is the equilibration of motion, healthful activity." And again, "In Life-unfoldment, the progress is from Black to Red—Red is the Zenith of manhood's prime; in the decline of Life the course is from Red to Black; in both unfoldment and decline, White is traversed, the healthful, elastic period of first maturity and of the medium stage of old age."

Pancoast worked in a rather simple way. Sunlight was made to pass through panes of red or blue glass—the two chief therapeutic agencies. "To ACCELERATE the Nervous System, in all cases of relaxation, the RED ray must be used, and to RELAX the Nervous System, in all cases of excessively accelerated tension, the BLUE ray must be used." According to his own word he effected a great number of miraculous cures and quoted numerous case histories.

Pleasanton, Pancoast and Babbitt were all condemned as charlatans as the years went by. Today, however, the skeptics are not so sure. There are different biological and physiological reactions to red and to blue—without doubt, as will be pointed out elsewhere in this book. And since psychosomatic medicine admits that psychological and emotional factors are medically significant, the mystic is not such a fakir as many have supposed.

Now as to Edwin D. Babbitt, his masterwork is fascinating to read, what for all its assumptions and conclusions. One most remarkable feature is his description and illustration of the atom (65 years before Hiroshima). Writing of "spirals" and "Spirillae," of "negative end vortex" and "positive end torrent," he amazingly forecast the atom and hydrogen bomb of a later decade. Colors were involved, red, orange, yellow, blue, violet. Consider the following remarkable statement from his *Principles*.

> Atoms indeed are the eggs out of which the whole universe is built, though on quite another principle. Their activities are so amazing that if one of them could be enlarged to the size of a man's head, constructed of some material millions of times stronger than anything known upon earth, and the tremendous whirl of forces set to revolving through their spirals which at their ordinary speed vibrate several hundred trillion times a second, what must be the effect? If such an atom should be set in the midst of New York City, it must create such a whirlwind that all its palatial structures, ships, bridges and surrounding cities, with nearly two millions of people, would be swept into fragments and carried into the sky.

Babbitt quotes many case histories of cures through color. Red "baths" were prescribed for paralysis, consumption, physical exhaustion, nervous prostration. Yellow and orange were prescribed as an emetic, laxative, purgative. Yellow was prescribed for costiveness, bronchial trouble, hemorrhoids. Yellow with some red was a cerebral stimulant, a good tonic in general. Blue and violet were prescribed for sciatica, inflammation, hemorrhage of the lungs, cerebro-spinal meningitis, neuralgic headache, nervousness, rheumatism, tumors in infants.

Such color therapy was bitterly denounced, and color healers and their equipment were confiscated or declared illegal.

To proceed with Babbitt, let me refer to his Chromolume, a device which he illustrated in black and white. Difficult if not impossible to reproduce in full color in his day (because of inadequate engraving techniques), a separate illustration shows the Chromolume and describes its transparent colors. Babbitt made this healing device available from his Science Hall ($10.00 for the large size, $9.00 for the smaller). (See page 111.)

Here follow Babbitt's own description and use of the Chromolume as set forth in his book.

THE CHROMOLUME

1. Having ascertained the color potencies which are transmitted through various hues of glass, as well as of fluids, we are now prepared to inquire how they should be combined in order best to harmonize with physiological law in the cure of human ailments.

2. *The Head and Brain.* In the first place the head being the positive battery of the whole system, and the brain having seven or eight times the amount of blood in proportion to its size that is averaged in other parts of the body, together with a great mass of nerve matter, its general tendency is to be especially warm and sensitive, consequently we need for its purpose the nerve-and-blood soothing colors, such as blue, indigo and violet, and the absence of the warm colors. For this reason panes of glass colored by the cupro-sulphate of ammonia would be most admirable for this purpose, especially as it gives free passage to the violet, indigo and blue rays, and almost entirely excludes the thermal, red, orange and yellow. The Mazarine blue glass, although handsome, is more heating as we have seen than other grades of blue, and therefore poorly adapted to the brain. Theoretically, the violet ray being the most refined and cooling, would naturally be the best for the head, but there is no violet glass known that can give us the pure violet without a goodly share of red, and this interferes with the best effect for most brains, for which reason the blue and indigo shades are on the whole the best. We will need, then, 12 or 15 inches of depth of the cooling style of blue glass to cover the head well, while its horizontal width may be about 15 inches. This we will form into a graceful ogee curve at the top, and for the sake of developing its power best will place a border of red orange, 2 or 3 inches in width, over its top and sides, to arouse its best affinitive action and give beauty of effect.

3. *The Neck and Thorax.* Joining immediately on to the last named glass, we shall need another piece for the neck and upper thorax, reaching considerably over the lungs and heart. This like the other should be cooling in its nature, being over a somewhat excitable region, and yet can well tolerate a certain amount of heat, so under ordinary circumstances the mazarine blue glass,

1. Light yellow colored with silver for the disc, 3 inches in diameter.
2,2. Light colored violet (manganese).
3,3. Red-orange (silver), 17 inches long.
4. The cool grade of blue, 14 inches deep by 16 broad, colored by cupro-sulphate of ammonia, or similar materials.
5. Mazarine blue, 6x16 inches, colored with cobalt.
6,6. Ruby-red on the left and gold-red on the right, 2-1/2x16 inches.
7. Purple, 6x16 inches, manganese and gold.
8,8. Light greenish-yellow, 2-1/2x6 inches, colored with uranium oxide.
9. Yellow, 3x16 inches, colored with iron or other metal.
10,10. Deep violet, 2-1/2x3 inches, manganese.
11. Green, 6x16 inches.
12,12. Dark red, 2-1/2x6 inches.
13. Orange 16-1/2x16 inches.
14,14. Light violet, 2-1/2x16 inches.
15. Red-orange, 2-1/2x16 inches, silver.
16,16. Blue, 2-1/2x2-1/2 inches.

The Chromolume, as illustrated and described by Edwin D. Babbitt. It consisted of a framed window with colored glass in different panels. One size, 21x57 inches, sold for ten dollars, with an extra dollar charged for boxing. Placed in a south orientation, and adjusted with cords "to make the light strike in the right place," wonders could be performed.

colored with cobalt, will probably be the very best which could be employed for that region. We will need about six inches of this and will border it with red, colored with gold.

4. *The Hypochondrium.* We come now to the upper bowels, including the liver, stomach, spleen, duodenum, etc., and constituting the central region of *digestion*. What color is most needed for good digestion? Two important substances are used in digesting food, gastric juice and saliva. The gastric juice being an acid, and consequently electrical, would have its action increased by the thermal colors, such as red and yellow, and the same colors would also stimulate the blood, muscles and nerves of the stomach, while the saliva, having the alkaline or thermal principle predominant, would have its chemical action increased by the blue or violet, which would also tend to counteract too much of the inflammatory action of the red. A medium purple glass transmits these principles and thus becomes par excellence the color for regulating digestion. Six inches of this will answer, and a border of yellow or greenish yellow, especially the canary yellow of uranium, will form its chemical affinity.

5. *The Umbilical Region.* The bowels are aroused into animation by the yellow color more especially, as has been abundantly shown, and a small strip of yellow glass three inches in depth, bordered by its affinitive violet, will be sufficient.

6. *The Hypogastrium and Loins.* For the loins and lower viscera, a green glass will have a fine tonic effect, and will be very soothing to any inflammatory conditions, such as cystitis, uterine or ovarian irritation, etc. Nearly every variety of green glass transmits the orange, yellow, green and blue rays. The yellow and orange will animate the nerves, while the blue will have a cooling effect and tend to constrict and draw up relaxed muscles. If the parts are dormant, yellow-green would be preferable—if inflamed and over-active, blue-green. A border glass of dark red will be nearly a chemical affinity.

7. *Lower Limbs.* For the rest of the way covering the limbs and lower extremities, the warmest colors are most desirable, especially as these parts are farthest from the vital centres. Having ascertained that the warmest effect comes through the orange or red-orange glass, this will be the most proper material, while the mazarine blue and the cooler blue will be excellent affinitive colors for the border on each side. About 15 inches of this will be sufficient, as the patient should sit or recline while receiving the colors.

8. The whole of this combination enclosed in a walnut frame with metallic frame work inside for the different colors, I have

termed the CHROMOLUME, which means literally color-light. Its colors being arranged very much on the law of harmonic contrast, as well as according to the principles of chemical affinity, it constitutes one of the most beautiful ornaments imaginable for a drawing-room, or bed-room window, and certainly one of the best of all instruments for vitalizing, healing and toning up the human system.

THE USE OF THE CHROMOLUME IN HEALING

1. *Positioning of the Instrument.* The lower end may rest upon the lower ledge of a window, while a cord is attached to the upper end, and being passed through an improvised loop at the top of the window may come down and be held by the hand, or wound around some hook or nail at the side of the window. In this way the upper end of the chromolume may be allowed to hang some distance from the window or parallel to the window to make the light strike in the right place, or the whole instrument may be drawn up further towards the top as circumstances may require. An invalid chair in which a person may be placed at different angles would be desirable, but an ordinary lounge or rocking chair will answer.

2. *Treatment of Head.* A majority of persons who are in feeble health, or who use the brain too intensely, have the head too warm, and the liver, stomach, and bowels too dormant, and the arrangement of the colored glass in the chromolume as already described, is just suited to such conditions. In case the brain and nerves, however, are in the negative condition which induces facial neuralgia and general coldness, the instrument should be raised a little, so that the face and ears at least should come in the range of the mazarine glass.

3. *Treatment on the Skin.* Decided benefit can be received from sitting in the light of the chromolume with the ordinary clothes on, much more benefit by sitting in a white garment or covered by a sheet, and still more benefit by allowing the rays to fall directly upon the skin. In this last case a person takes a full air bath as well as a color bath. With dark clothes on, the light is degraded into mere heat, although of a fine quality.

4. *Treatment of the Back.* After using the light in front for some time, the patient should turn over and let it strike on the back in much the same manner as on the front. If the back of the neck and lower spine and hips are especially cold, the patient should slip down farther into the warm rays, the upper spine and occiput coming under the mazarine glass, and the lower spine coming under the orange and green glass combined. By animating the

occiput, and the cervical and brachial plexuses of nerves, reaching as low as the shoulders, a life-giving power is communicated to the arms, lungs, motor nerves, etc., which will prevent, or tend to cure, rheumatic, paralytic, or inflammatory conditions of those parts, while by thoroughly animating the lumbar and sacral plexuses of the lower spine, the lower viscera and limbs will receive a new life, and sciatica, lumbago, rheumatism, gout, paralysis, etc., be relieved. In female or other difficulties which cause the small of the back to be hot and weak, that portion should be under the green glass, and the hips, which are apt to be cold, under the orange. The green, which is one of the most cooling of all glasses will thus tone up the back, while the orange glass, by its great heat, will call away the warmth from above, and animate those nerves that give warmth to limbs and feet, which in such cases are generally too cold.

5. *White Light with the Colored.* In most baths of the chromo-lume light, it would be well for a part of the time *to have a portion of the body under the direct sunlight,* keeping the head in most cases in the blue light, or if even that is too strong for a very sensitive brain, the light can be shut off altogether from the head, by hanging cloth or paper over the upper part of the instrument. If a correct anti-thermal blue glass can be found, such a precaution will not be necessary.

6. *If the bowels are habitually too free or inflamed,* the narrow strip of the yellow glass can be covered up, and the body slipped down farther under the green, the tendency of which is cooling, anti-inflammatory, and constricting.

7. *For sluggish action of the kidneys,* tendency to dropsical affections, Bright's disease, etc., it would be well to have the junction of the yellow and purple glass come just above the small of the back, remembering also to have the white light fall on that portion for a time each day, especially the white and colored light combined.

8. *For Feverish and Irregular Condition of the Sexual System,* the green glass light should come over the small of the back and lower spine, the orange commencing at the lower part of the hips. This rule is of great importance, and will tend to save the patient from the fearful wreck that overtakes vast multitudes of mankind, and from a condition which, if not arrested in time, will baffle the power of all drugs to heal. It should be pursued perseveringly, days, weeks and months if necessary, for there is a quiet, deep-reaching and marvelous power in well regulated light to heal all such difficulties, as well as to build up exhausted nervous systems generally.

9. *Artificial light* may be used to fine advantage with the chromolume, especially if the lamp or gas-burner is directly behind the blue or green shades of glass. Such lights having a larger relative amount of carbon than sun-light, the yellow and orange principles are more active, which fact explains the cause of their being more exciting to the eyes and nervous system than the light of day, causing inflammation of the eyes (ophthalmia), dimness of vision (amaurosis), etc. Blue and violet light constitutes a beautiful balancing power for such conditions. The great advantage of being able to use artificial light, especially in a country like England, in which direct sunlight in winter is very scarce, and also during the darker portions of our own year, must be apparent to all. Artificial light has much the same character as sunlight, with the exception that it is feebler, less white, and more irritating, but when it is purified by being strained through glass, and its yellowish and reddish character offset by a certain amount of the blue and violet element, it can be made very valuable. The electric light has great power and purity. Although the light for general purposes may well be placed directly back of the blue glass, yet for special conditions it must be changed; thus, for head-ache, sleeplessness, etc., place it back of the upper blue; for sore throat, and most lung difficulties, place it back of the mazarine blue; for indigestion, back of the purple; for costiveness, back of the yellow; for uterine or ovarian inflammation, back of the green, etc.

10. *A convex Lens for concentrating the rays,* hung behind any particular kind of glass, according to the part of the body which needs most power, greatly intensifies and hastens the action of the light, but this should not generally be done over the brain, or over the heart in case it is subject to palpitation.

Babbitt seemed mighty sure of the particular healing effects of different colors. While what he had to say was highly exaggerated—and questionable—it was not mere nonsense. As will be pointed out later, red light and blue light have therapeutic applications today in recognized and approved medical circles. While there is little doubt as to the efficiency of infrared and ultraviolet radiation, what has been noted quite recently is that *visible* light too has its benefits and will successfully treat various afflictions.

In Babbitt's day, people kept out of the sun. He wrote,

Many persons keep themselves pale and sickly by means of parasols, umbrellas, shaded rooms, and in-door life generally.

Parasols should be dispensed with excepting in the hottest seasons. Sailors who are ever in the pure air and sunlight, and children who play much out of doors, generally present a ruddy, healthy appearance. The following severe cut on our American house-keepers, from an editorial of the Chicago Tribune, is well merited:—

"In this country, there seems to be an implacable feud between people and the sun—the one striving vigorously and even fiercely to get into the houses, and the other striving just as fiercely and vigorously to keep him out. The Average American housekeper does not think she has fulfilled her whole duty until she has made the rounds of the whole household, shut all the doors, closed all the shutters, and drawn all the curtains on the east and south sides of the house. This is the morning's job. In the afternoon she makes the same grand round on the west side of the house. She is not quite happy and contented until the sun has gone down and darkness sets in. She is substantially aided in her raid against the sunlight by the heaviest of shades, curtains and lambrequins. Thus the fight goes on day by day and season by season. In summer she shuts out the sun because it is too hot. In winter she shuts it out because it will spoil her carpets. In spring and fall she has other reasons. She has reasons for all seasons. Thus she keeps the house in perpetual shade, in which the children grow up sickly, dwarfed, full of aches and pains, and finally have to be sent off into the country post-haste so that they may get into that very sunlight which they have been denied at home, and in which the country children run and are glorified."

The bathing beauty of 1878 wore a sailor blouse with sleeves, bloomers, stockings, cap. Beauty in women demanded a fair skin. Anyone with a coat of tan had to be a laborer or farmer's wife, for no true lady would allow her skin to be discolored.

Babbitt advised people to expose themselves to sunlight—and maybe this is what resulted in many cures. With considerable emotion he wrote,

The ancients often had terraces, called *Solaria,* built on the tops of their houses, where they were in the habit of taking their solar air baths. Pliny says that for 600 years Rome had no physicians. Using such natural methods of retaining or gaining physical power as vapor baths, manipulation, sunlight, exercise, etc., they became the mightiest of nations. By this remark I throw out no slur against true and wise physicians, who are blessings to a community, but would call their attention more to nature's finer methods rather than to the use of so many drugs, blisters, moxas, bleedings, leechings, and other violent processes which so weaken and destroy the beautiful temple of the human body.

THE EMPRESS.

XI

Color Therapy Today

In my work as a professional color consultant I have been called upon to justify the use of color in habitats where difficult tasks may be performed and where human welfare is to be safeguarded. This does not concern homes, but industrial plants, offices, schools, hospitals, neuropsychiatric facilities. To substantiate what I do, I pay close attention to research in vision, physiology, and psychology. I then apply in practical ways what the pure scientist has concluded as to effects for color.

Where colleagues of mine may deny all or most claims for color therapy, I merely smile and continue on my way. With mental patients, for example, if there are no effects for color, should institutions be painted gray or ivory?

This chapter has to do with biological and physiological responses to color. In following chapters reference will be made to auras and emanations, to psychological and emotional reactions, and to inimical effects that follow *lack* of exposure to color.

Direct biological and physiological reactions to color can be quoted by the score—all personal feelings in the matter quite aside. How do human beings (plants, animals) respond to color, consciously or unconsciously?

To start with plants and lower forms of life, considerable

119

The Enraged Quacks, from a late 18th century engraving. Charlatanism
in healing has often been associated with color. This unfortunately has
tended to deny therapeutic benefits for visible light and color. Today,
however, the medical profession has accepted many forms of color
therapy, and more recognition is sure to come.

research has been performed. Among the prominent investigators of plants have been H. A. Borthwick of the U.S. Department of Agriculture, Stuart Dunn of the University of New Hampshire and R. van der Veen and G. Meijer of the Philips Research Laboratories in Holland. It was Borthwick who noted an antagonism between visible red light and invisible infrared. Red would cause lettuce seed to sprout, for example, while infrared would put the sprouts back to sleep. Similarly, red would inhibit the flowering of the short-day plants and promote that of long-day ones. Van der Veen and Meijer reported that there was maximum absorption of red light and, hence, maximum plant action. Blue also had its effects, but yellow and green were neutral or reduced activity, while short ultra-violet would destroy the plant.

What is unusual is that plants seem most responsive to red and blue and are inactive to yellow and yellow-green. The human eye, however, finds maximum sensitivity (visibility) to yellow and yellow-green. In a greenhouse under artificial light, weak green illumination is "safe" light for plants, for there is little if any plant response to it. This light is to the plant physiologist "what the ruby light was for the photographer."

Stuart Dunn's findings in the growth of tomato seedlings are particularly interesting. "The yield by the warm white lamps was highest of all the commercially available fluorescent lamps. Next to it stood that of the blue and pink lamps. Green and red were low. The experimental 'high intensity' of red lamps produced the highest yield of all. Stem growth (elongation) is promoted especially by the yellow part of the spectrum." However, "Succulence is increased by the long wavelengths (red) and decreased by blue light." In France, the irradiation of potato plants with red light has stimulated germination, and satisfactory crop yields have been achieved. Growing flowering plants completely under artificial light is fast becoming a national hobby in the United States, making the mystery and magic of color more impressive to the layman.

For the most part, insects have a fair sense of color, being insensitive to red but sensitive to yellow, green, blue, violet and into ultraviolet, which is invisible to man. A group of researchers, H. B. Weiss, F. A. Soroci and E. E. McCoy Jr., tested about 4,500 insects, mostly beetles, and found that 72 percent reacted positively to some wavelength, 33 percent to yellow-green, 14 percent to violet-blue, 11 percent to blue and 11 percent to ultra-violet. Few showed any attraction to warm colors. "It thus appears that in general the shorter wavelengths of light are more stimulating and attractive, whereas the longer wavelengths are considerably less stimulative and perhaps repellent in nature to coleopterous [beetles] forms of life."

In a study performed for the US Atomic Energy Commission in 1968, three researchers investigated the influence of visible colors on voluntary activity in albino RF-strain mice. The rodents were placed in cubicles for periods of 18 hours, rested and then were placed for 18 hours in other cubicles until all environments were tested. The measure of activity was determined by the revolutions of activity wheels, similar to those seen in squirrel cages. Mice are nocturnal animals and hence are most active in darkness, as results of the test showed. Next greatest activity was with red. The RF-strain mouse experiences red as darkness. "Activity in yellow light was significantly greater than in daylight, green, blue and significantly less than in dark and red." Incidentally, blind mice showed little difference in activity, regardless of color, bearing out that the effects discovered were "due to visual receptors." While mice and men are not to be confused, the story bore out the fact that different colors have different effects.

Recently, *visible* blue light has been found to counteract jaundice in newborn infants caused by an excess of bilirubin in the blood. Complete blood exchange may be prescribed, but phototherapy is also effective. Researchers Luke Thorington, L. Cunningham and J. Parascondola have commented in an article: "It is evident that all radiation near 555mn in yellow-green is most effective for producing 'light,' while that near 410–460mn in the violet and blue is most effective for 'bleaching and degrading' serum bilirubin, which results in the basic difference in 'light' requirements of the engineer and phototherapist." There is true color therapy in this particular instance.

Then there is the matter of photosensitivity. In 1900 Oscar Raab of Munich published a number of important findings on the toxicity of dyes. Experimenting with different dye solutions, he discovered that the time required to destroy microscopic organisms was related both to the intensity of light in his laboratory and to the density of his dyestuffs. Organisms exposed to sunlight might survive over long periods. However, when dye was introduced the organism could be made sensitive to light and promptly killed.

Raab's work led to much subsequent research. Dyes and pigments could be used to sensitize a wide variety of living organisms. While the dye itself might be chemically inert, it stained the microbe, caused light to be absorbed, and resulted in death.

With reference to this phenomenon, substances which are fluorescent in solution are likely to have the most intense action. What happens is that the dye causes different (and perhaps unfavorable) wavelengths to be absorbed. Although absorption of ultraviolet is harmful, so also is absorption of visible light, for investigations have shown that such metabolic effects can be achieved with visible light alone.

Any number of dyes and substances can be used to make an organism (or human skin) sensitive to light. Eosin, a red dye, has been added to milk to treat rachitic children on the principle that ultraviolet radiation will be more readily absorbed. Rose bengal and methylene blue will cause particular sensitivity to green and yellow light.

Strange skin eruptions may follow the use of cosmetics, ointments, perfumes, after-shave lotions. Frequently associated with poisoning, such "diseases" are often to be attributed to the fact that the substances make the skin light-sensitive and, in effect, aggravate "sunburn."

The red blood cells of mammals, suspended in salt solution, will withstand sunlight for several hours without appreciable change if exceedingly short wave lengths are excluded. However, where a fluorescent dye may be added, an almost immediate damage to the cell structure will be noted.

The introduction of dyes will also inactivate a long list of toxins, antitoxins, viruses, and venoms. Hormones may likewise be destroyed. "Human skin may be locally sensitized by photodynamic dyes . . . and in this case intense itching occurs when the sensitized part is exposed to light" (Blum).

It may well be that certain forms of "hives," such as "strawberry rash," represent instances in which the eating of certain foods make the skin light-sensitive. As a case in point, a great amount of study has been given to the effect of buckwheat in the diet of animals. In fact, many diseases of animals may be traced to light sensitivity brought about by eating certain foods.

Both in Arabia and Australia sheep have been painted—with good success—on the theory that dark animals seem to be less troubled with certain afflictions than light ones. In practically all cases of sensitivity to light, animals with the least pigmented skin are most affected.

There are also many instances in which contact with certain substances may cause eruptions. The chlorophyll of ordinary grass, crushed onto the skin, may produce lesions if the person rolls over and exposes the area of skin to sunlight. The handling of parsnips and figs may produce dermatitis. Coal-tar products may represent an occupational hazard to some individuals. Many workers handling coal-tar products find themselves extremely sensitive to light.

On this relation between pigmentation and reaction to light, L. Roule has presented an unusual theory regarding the migration of salmon. At the end of the second year, the young fish begins to lose pigment from its skin. This results in an irritating effect as strong sunlight penetrates shallow water, and drives the salmon downstream and into the sea. "Very probable this is not the only factor in bringing about the movement. However, it appears significant that the trout, a close relative which loses much less pigment than does the salmon, remains in fresh water" (Maier and Schneirla).

There is a strange and rare condition of photosensitivity in human beings known as urticaria solare. It offers striking evidence of the biological effect of visible light, for in urticaria solare visible blue and violet light are the undoubted cause of the ailment. The amount of sunlight necessary to produce this skin affliction (called "triple response" by Blum) is very small. In one case an exposure of three minutes produced a definite discoloration and swelling. "It is safe to say that this response occurs in skins which are otherwise apparently normal, because of the presence of a photoactive substance which absorbs in the blue and violet regions of the spectrum. This substance is probably not present in normal skins, although it may be present but not active under normal circumstances." In experiments conducted by Blum and others, blue and violet light, which had been isolated with the aid of color and temperature filters, still produced the erythema of urticaria solare. All too clearly this minor affliction is one that is aggravated by visible blue and violet light, not by heat rays or ultraviolet rays. Though it may be exceedingly rare to medical science, it should admonish the skeptic and remind him that visible light and color are not without action on the human body.

Today certain photosensitizing chemicals, taken orally, have been found to make diseased tissue particularly sensitive to visible and long wave ultraviolet light. Psoriasis can be relieved. This type of therapy is being employed to treat some forms of superficial tumors and cancer.

Mysticism and occultism may not be greatly involved, if at all, in biological effects for color such as described in this chapter. However, modern research does support much of the confidence of mystics of old that color has magic indeed. And each year, more data on unique effects for color are released from the cautious sanctums of science.

In *Germs and Man,* Justina Hill refers to the ancient use of compounds of mercury, silver and copper. "These dyes exhibit marked preferences in their antiseptic action for different groups of organisms." Cinnabar (the red sulfide of mercury), "ye blood of ye dragon," was prescribed for eye diseases, burns and pustules. In the form of mercurochrome in aqueous solution, it still continues to be used.

In some instances the ancient credited his miracles to color rather than to the chemical properties of his nostrums. Thus the purple dye extracted from murex shells was used to check the overgrowth of granulation tissue and to draw pus from boils. What the ancient failed to realize was "that this efficacy was unrelated to the glorious color of the purpura, but due to the formation of calcium oxide, one of the first compounds which was to lead to Dakin's solution 2,000 years later."

XII

The Significance of Astral Light

Here is further material drawn largely from my book, *The Story of Color*. With three chapters, let this first one tell of the mystic approach, with little regard for hyperbole and fancy. Let the second chapter then be a bridge between the occult and that which holds the probability of validity. Then let the third chapter present more positive evidence as to the reality of the aura, supporting its premises with the recordings of modern scientific equipment—the polygraph and electroencephalograph.

In the mystic approach, all early civilizations used color as tokens of the loftier qualities of human culture. There were certain philosophers, however, who went beyond the formal symbolism of the Mysteries and studied the auric light that was thought to issue from the body. Here the true marks of culture were to be found, as unmistakable as the rainbow, visible, actual, and the real index to a man's inherent qualities, good and bad.

Man had been likened to a celestial body emitting vibrations of light. This concept usually referred to the sun or to a supreme invisible deity whose rays gave life and spirit to humans. The halos, robes, insignia, jewels, and ornaments used upon their own persons and upon the effigies of their gods symbolized the spiritual energies that radiated from the body. The elaborate headdress of the Egyptian and the nimbus of the Christian saint represented the auric bodies of the elect. These streams were supposed to pour from the surface of the flesh, and their colors were a gauge of cultural development, spiritual perfection, and physical health.

To the mystic all plants and animals emitted an aura. (This has been confirmed in modern times.) In man the aura was as much a part of his entity as his body. Celebrated men like Benvenuto Cellini had noted it. "Ever since the time of my strange vision until now an aureole of glory (marvelous to relate) has rested on my head. This is visible to every sort of men to whom I have chosen to point it out; but there have been very few. This halo can be observed above my shadow in the morning from the rising of the sun for about two hours, and far better when the grass is drenched with dew."

Now just as the brain was said by the occultist to be the central organ for the circulation of nerve-fluid, and as the heart was the central organ for the circulation of blood, the spleen was the organ from which the astral elements drew their vitality. The emanations, in consequence, were affected by the physical, emotional, and spiritual state of the body. Colors differed as individuals differed and also as the mood and thought of any one person underwent change. Franz Hartmann writes: "The quality of psychic emanations depends on the state of activity of the center from which they originate, for each thing and each being is tinctured with that particular principle which exists at the invisible center, and from this center receives the form of its own character or attributes."

Rather involved. Yet the mystic insisted that the true character of men was shown in their auras. In persons of low nature the predominating color was dark red. In persons of high nature the hues were white and blue, gold and green, in various tints. Red indicated desire. Blue indicated love. Green indicated benevolence.

Swami Panchadasi writes: "The human aura may be described as a fine, ethereal tradition or emanation surrounding each and every human being. It extends from two to three feet, in all directions, from the body." It may be likened to the rising of heat

This dramatic painting by Matthias Gruenwald, early 16th century, portrays the Resurrection and Transformation of Jesus and is from the Isenheim Alterpiece. Radiating from the head of Jeses is an aura of yellow, gold, orange in a field of deep blue. (Unterlinden Museum, Colmar, France. Photograph by O. Zimmerman.)

from a stove. The colors of the aura are said to be best seen by those having psychic insight. They fluctuate and change. They may be tranquil like water or impulsive like flames. They will reveal peace of heart and flash deep rays of anger and hatred.

In form, some of the hues are soft and misty. Others shoot out in straight lines. Still others unfold like coils. C. W. Leadbeater in his *Man, Visible and Invisible* described the significance of these emanations.

Black clouds indicate hatred and malice.

Deep flashes of red on a black ground show anger. A sanguine red exposes an unmistakable sensuality.

A dull brown means avarice. A grayish brown means selfishness. A greenish brown means jealousy.

Gray is to be associated with depression and fear.

Crimson shows a loving nature.

Orange reveals pride and ambition.

Yellow emanates from the aura of the intellectual person.

A grayish green signifies deceit and cunning. An emerald green shows versatility and ingenuity. A pale, delicate green means sympathy and compassion.

Dark blue shines forth from the person having great religious feeling. Light blue indicates devotion to noble ideals.

Thus the character of humans reads like a Neon sign for the elect. The aura of the savage is dull yellow over his head and shows rays of grayish blue, dull orange and the brownish red of sensuality. All the colors are irregular in outline. The average person emits hues of a higher octave, more yellow, pure red, and clear blue. In anger black swirls and flashes of red are seen. In fear there is a livid gray mist. In devotion the colors are bluish.

Floating specks of scarlet issue from the irritable man. The miser is exposed by deep brownish bars of light. The depressed soul sends forth dull gray rays. The devotional type has an aura greatly developed in blue.

Finally, the aura of the superman is filled with iridescent hues: "All the colors of an Egyptian sunset and the softness of an English sky at eventide." There is a yellow nimbus about his head.

By these tokens the innate personality of a being is divulged. Yet beyond this, the colors of the astral spectrum may have a higher complexity.

The primary astral hues are red, yellow, and blue. Black is the absence of color. White is the harmonious blending of all colors.

Red is the physical phase of mentality. It indicates health, vigor, friendship, love. The baser qualities show themselves in deep shades of red.

Yellow is the intellectual phase of being. Golden yellow is the highest form.

Blue is the religious or spiritual phase. The higher form is a violet tint. The lower form is an indigo shade.

Orange is the union of mind and body, a sign of sound wisdom and justice.

Green marks the lover of nature. It is indicative of sympathy, altruism, charity. Slate-green is a telling symbol of jealousy and deceit.

Violet exposes a love of form and ceremony. Here is the union of spirit and body (blue and red), a symbol of great ideality and sublimity.

Black is the negation of spirit, the negative pole of being.

White reveals the Pure Spirit, the positive pole of being. White transcends all other lights and signifies the perfect degree of spiritual attainment and unfoldment.

Babbitt in his celebrated book on color presented a good deal of material on the work of Mrs. Minnie Weston as to the psychic colors that are said to issue from the brain. These hues comprise what Babbitt termed the odic atmosphere. He pointed out, first of all, a need for harmony between the vibrations of the world and the human body and recommends that a person should sleep with his head at the north to "lie in the magnetic meridian." (The worst position is with the head at the west.)

Odic light appears in five forms—as incandescence, as flame, as threads, streaks or nebulae, as smoke, and as sparks. The odic atmosphere is thought to be twice as fine as ordinary atmosphere, because its vibrations are twice as fine as those of light.

Generally the vulgar brain emits brownish, deep red, and blackish colors. The higher brain emits clear yellowish tints and far more brilliance.

In the higher brain, there is blue over the brow. Benevolence is shown by a soft green light. Firmness emits scarlet. Self-esteem emits purple. To quote Babbitt: "The region of Religious aspiration, pointing heavenward, is the sun-realm of the human soul, and the most luminous of all, being a person of noble and spiritual nature of an exquisite golden yellow, approaching a pure and dazzling white. The front brain being the realm of Reason and Perception, manifests itself naturally in the cool and calm color, blue, while the love principle, typified all over the world by warmth, finds its natural manifestation in red. Such faculties as those of Ideality, Spirituality, and Sublimity, combining as they do both thought and emotion, radiate the violet, or the union of blue and red, while such faculties as Patience, Firmness, Integrity and Temperance, have more to do with coolness than heat, and have a predominance of the blue."

Some occultists tell of an astral world where culture reigns supreme. It is inhabited by the nature-spirits of Paracelsus, the undines (water spirits), the sylphs (air spirits), the gnomes (earth spirits), and the salamanders (fire spirits). Fortunately or unfortunately they seldom chose to visit the mortal haunts of men.

C. W. Leadbeater says, "Under ordinary conditions they are not visible to physical sight at all, but they have the power of making themselves so by materialization when they wish to be seen."

The astral world itself, which is likened to the celestial realms of the Atlanteans, Greeks, and Christians, is indeed beautiful to behold in fancy. Hartmann says, "Wherever a man's consciousness is, there is the man himself, no matter whether his physical body is there or not." In Panchadasi's book this world is described as having seven planes graded according to degrees of vibration. These planes are to be attained by those having an astral sense. How fortunate the man who reaches them! Hartmann declares, "He who can see the images existing in the Astral Light can read the history of all past events and prophesy the future!" For here culture reaches the true Golden Age that has been the dream of mankind since the beginning of time.

Recently the trance medium, Edgar Cayce, declared that he saw color surrounding most persons. His interpretations, however, were conventionally those of the mystic. Red was for force, vigor and energy; orange was for thoughtfulness and consideration; yellow for health and well-being; green was the color of healing; blue was the color of the spirit; indigo and violet indicated those searching for religious experience. Like his predecessors he wrote, "The perfect color, of course, is white, and this is what we are all striving for. If our souls were in perfect balance, then all our color vibrations would blend and we would have an aura of pure white."

With good prescience, Edgar Cayce saw great practical value in the study of the aura. It could be interpreted for purposes of diagnosis and therapy—and this will be seen in chapters that follow. He cautioned, "But I do not think that color therapy will become widespread or practical until we have accepted the truth of auras and become accustomed to reading them in order to discover what unbalance is disturbing a person."

THE CHARIOT.

XIII

The Aura, Transition from Past to Present

It is natural perhaps but unfortunate that a great deal of modern medical science persists in being at loggerheads with all principles of divine healing. Yet one is not to doubt the verity of miraculous cures. Though diseases for the most part may be born of germs, this does not even imply that man is helpless to thwart them except through so-called scientific means. The body in good health resists contamination, and psychiatry demonstrates that the mind in good health will to a considerable extent preserve the body.

Unquestionably there is something psychic in the art of healing, something akin to the supernatural. The will to live is itself an effective remedy. But beyond this it is entirely likely that ancient healers did effect astonishing cures. How? Was there intercession from the deity or did the ritual of the healer so inspire the patient as to give him the necessary "medicine" to thrill him to recovery? It is known today that mental disturbances produce physical ones. If affliction may work in this fashion, then the process is to be reversed—mental calm may assist in restoring bodily calm.

135

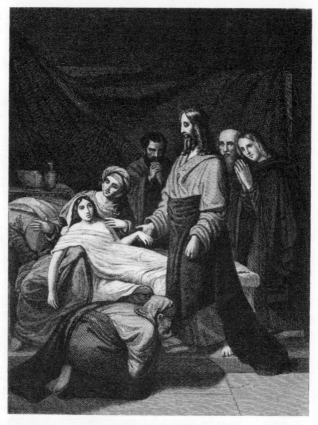

Matthew, Mark and Luke all refer to the miracle healing of the daughter
of Jairus by Jeses. "Somebody hath touched me: for I perceive that virtue
is gone out of me." The healing properties of emenations from the
bodies of some gifted persons have been accepted and acknowledged for
centuries. Modern medicine is obliged to admit psychic factors in
healing.

In color is a psychic factor, appealing, emotional, in every way inspiring and suggestive of mysterious powers. Thus before discussing what modern medicine is willing to admit about color and the aura, this chapter will offer a convenient and logical shift from the occult viewpoint to the clinical.

The study of the human aura and of astral light is not always a matter of mysticism and abracadabra. Even the most incredulous person is forced to admit that an emanation of some sort issues from the human body. This can not only be sensed as heat or odor but under proper conditions it can actually be seen. Sir Oliver Lodge wrote, "All evidence tends to convince me that we have an Etheric body as well as a physical body . . . it is the organized entity that builds up the body."

The human aura is affected by the physical condition of the body. Its manifestations are concerned with health and consequently with healing. To certain passionately inspired mystics astral light is a healing force. It represents the divine emanations of the deity shining from within the body of man. Auras are said to flow from the holy buildings of the Orientals and Mohammedans, more so than from the temples of the Christians so many of whom disdain psychic phenomena. The hands of Christ may have healed because from them came emanations that flooded the being of the afflicted one. A person may sense the depression of the sick-room because of its somber vibrations.

Paracelsus credited the body with having two substances, invisible and visible. The latter substance, the etheric shadow, was beyond disintegration. Derangements of it produced disease. He therefore sought to reharmonize the substance by bringing it in contact with healthy bodies whose vital energy might supply the elements needed to overthrow the affliction.

The auric healer of the occult school worked in three ways, by thought-transference, by influencing the aura of the patient, and by encouraging the right emanations. In short he (a) set up vibrations in the mind of his patient through concentration; (b) his thought on certain hues will build up his own aura and thence act directly on the aura of his patient; (c) and this in turn will arouse corresponding vibrations in the mind of the patient—and effect the cure.

This auric healing is mental and spiritual rather than literal. No colored lights or colored mediums are employed. The whole process is a psychic one. Babbitt's theories are in reverse.

For the nervous system, the auric colors used in mental concentration are violet and lavender for a soothing effect, grass greens for an invigorating effect, and medium yellows and oranges for an inspiring effect.

For the blood and organs of the body, clear dark blues are soothing, grass greens are invigorating, and bright reds are stimulating. Blue was the hue to think about in cases of fever, high blood pressure or hysteria. Red was the hue in cases of chill or lack of sufficient bodily warmth.

Panchadasi writes: "A nervous, unstrung patient, may be treated by bathing him mentally, in a flood of violet or lavender auric color; while a tired, used up, fatigued person may be invigorated by flooding him with bright reds, followed by bright, rich yellows, finishing the treatment with a steady flow of warm orange color."

The concluding vibration will then be the Great White Light. "This will leave the patient in an inspired, exalted, illuminated state of mind and soul, which will be of great benefit to him, and will also have the effect of reinvigorating the healer by cosmic energy."

And lest the skeptical physician frown haughtily upon the therapy of auric healing, one stout champion utters this warning: "The purblind atheist scientists who practice vivisection, the injection of disgusting lymph and other abominable iniquities in the vain hope of annihilating disease by propagating it, must, sooner or later, be brought to see the error of their ways."

If the work of Babbitt is too fantastic for modern medicine, then the theories of auric healers of the past must seem ludicrous. Nonetheless, the aura can no longer be doubted, as the next chapter will tell. Nor can it be ignored if the healing science is to practice the sincerity it preaches.

There have been any number of devout investigators of the phenomenon who have been satisfied to report only what they have seen and experienced and to refrain from losing themselves to the vagaries of their imaginations. All admit that simple colors are visible to the eye. If a full array of hues, rivaling the sunset or the rainbow, is to be seen, one must indeed by psychic and a prodigy among men.

A bridge from the astral emanations of the mystic to the recognized energy fields by the modern scientists was crossed in principle as far back as the 17th century. In 1679 one William Maxwell

wrote a treatise, *De Medicina Magnetica,* in which he said the
following:

"Material rays flow from all bodies in which the soul operates
by its presence. By these rays energy and the power of working
are diffused. The vital spirit which descends from the sky, pure,
unchanged, and whole, is the parent of the vital spirit which
exists in all things. If you make use of the universal spirit by
means of instruments impregnated with this spirit you will
thereby call to your aid the great secret of the ages. The universal
medicine is nothing but the vital spirit repeated in the proper subject."

This assumption later inspired the great father of hypnotism,
Franz Anton Mesmer (1733?–1815). As described in my book
Color in Human Response, Mesmer became an expert in animal
magneticism, studied in Vienna and opened a famous clinic in
Paris which drew patients from all over Europe. In 1779 Mesmer
declared, "A mutual influence subsists between the celestial
bodies, the earth, and the living bodies."

What he devised was a magnetic tub, oval in shape, and surrounded by chairs or benches on which the patients sat. The con-
trivance was described at the time in these words:

"M. Mesmer, Doctor of Medicine of the Faculty of Vienna, in
Austria, is the sole discoverer of animal magnetism. This method
of curing a multitude of ailments—hydropsy, paralysis, gout,
scurvy, blindness, and accidental deafness among others—consists
in the application of a fluid or agent which M. Mesmer directs
upon those who resort to him, sometimes with one of his fingers
and sometimes with an iron rod held by another and pointed as he
chooses. He also employs a tub furnished with attached cords,
which the sick persons tie round themselves, and with bent-iron
bars, which they approach to the pit of their stomach, their liver,
or their spleen, or, in general, to any part of their body in which
they suffer. The sick persons, especially the females, go into convulsions or fits which bring about their cure. The Magnetizers
(they are those to whom M. Mesmer has revealed his secret, and
are more than a hundred in number, among them counting the
first nobles of the court) place their hands upon the part affected
and rub it for some time; this operation hastens the effect of the
cords and irons. Every other day there is a tub for the poor; in
the antechamber musicians play airs calculated to induce gaiety in
the sick persons. Men and women of every age and every degree

are seen arriving in crowds at this celebrated physician's house—
the soldier with his badges of honour, the lawyer, the monk, the
man of letters, the blue-ribbon cook, the artisan, the physician,
the surgeon. It is a spectacle truly worthy of feeling souls to see
men distinguished by birth or social rank magnetizing, with
tender solicitude, children, aged persons, and, above all, the
necessitous. As for M. Mesmer, he breathes an air of beneficence
in all his discourse; he is grave and speaks little. His head seems
always filled with great thoughts."

Mesmer's clientele was quite eminent. He could also magnetize
water and use it as a therapeutic elixir. Though he was praised by
some, others looked upon his work as that of the devil. Thus he
was a great benefactor and charlatan at one and the same time.

In modern times, a number of investigators have come upon
the auric scene. Let me refer to the work of George Starr White,
Walter J. Kilner and Oscar Bagnall.

The Story of the Human Aura, written by George Starr White
(1928), takes a fairly middle course between the eloquent
viewpoint of the mystic and the modest viewpoint of the scientist.
Agreeing with Mesmer, White declares that a magnetic atmosphere surrounds animals and plants. These emanations differ and
are subject to change. Accepting them, one may account for the
mysteries of thought-transference, the weird prescience of strange
happenings that often strike a person. He states that health and
disease make themselves evident in the aura. And the rays change
in appearance when a person is turned towards different points of
the compass. "No matter what form life or vital force may take,
no matter what vehicle life is carried in—be it animate or
inanimate—its magnetic atmosphere must be characteristic of the
vehicle."

White concludes that the magnetic emanations from the
forefinger of the left hand and the thumb of the right hand are
positive, and that the emanations from the forefinger of the right
hand and the thumb of the left hand are negative. He describes an
auric cabinet to study the phenomenon. The color of the average
aura is grayish blue. (Kirlian photography has now made actual
photographs of auras.)

A more logical and unprejudiced attitude, however, is to be
found in Walter J. Kilner's book, *The Human Atmosphere* (1911).
Kilner very deliberately shunned the mystic aspects of auric light

and made his investigation with all the sedulity of a laboratory worker. His conclusions: surrounding the human body is a visible envelope having three definite parts. First is a narrow dark band, a quarter of an inch wide, which is adjacent to the skin. Beyond this, and projecting from two to four inches outward, is a second aura. This is the clearest of all. And beyond this is a third aura, misty in aspect and without sharp outline on its farther edge. This is generally about six inches across.

Normally the radiations shoot out at right angles from the body. These rays are electric in appearance and have a fugitive quality, shifting and changing. Longer rays project from the fingers, the elbows, knees, hips, the breasts. The color of health is a bluish gray, according to Kilner, and tinged with yellow and red. A grayer and duller color is typical to a diseased body. Kilner, however, preferred to base his diagnoses on the shape of the aura rather than on its chromatic qualities.

Kilner's work was taken up and vastly improved by Oscar Bagnall. In *The Origin and Properties of the Human Aura* (1937) a number of engaging theories are set fourth, and also a detailed explanation as to the procedure to follow in making the aura visible. Some may observe it merely by gazing at a person in a dimly illuminated room. Bagnall, however, following the example of Kilner, makes use of a special screen.

He divides the aura into two parts, an inner and an outer. The inner aura, about three inches across, is marked by a clear brightness and rays that shoot out in straight lines. This aura is approximately the same in all persons. It may also be supplemented by special bundles of rays emanating from various parts of the body and not necessarily being parallel to the other rays.

The outer aura, more filmy, enlarges with age and generally has greater dimension in women than in men. Its average width is about six inches. Color is best seen here—bluish or grayish. The bluer the hue the finer the intellect. The grayer the tone the duller the intellect. The outer aura is subject to radical change brought about by mood or disease. Bagnall declares that no aura shines from any dead thing.

In studying the aura, the eye is first sensitized by gazing at the sky through a special dicyanin (blue) filter. The observer then sits with his back to the window. A feeble illumination is permitted to enter the room. The patient, naked, stands before a neutral screen.

According to Bagnall auric light has definite wavelengths that lie beyond the visible spectrum. Because blue and violet rays are seen better by the rods of the eye than by the cones, the blue filter tends to eliminate the longer red and orange rays of light and to emphasize the violet. Sensitizing of the eye can also be achieved by first gazing at areas of yellow paper which fatigue the retinal nerves to red and green and at the same time bring out a stronger response to blue.

In a fascinating theory Bagnall credits nocturnal birds and animals with special vision. Rod vision, so prevalent in animals, may add dimension to the sense of sight in many creatures, enabling them to see emanations which to the human eye are invisible. Certain insects can "see" ultraviolet radiation. Birds are particularly sensitive to red radiation. Some snakes have organs sensitive to heat rays and can locate living food in complete darkness.

But to return to mankind—organic diseases seem to affect the inner ura. The emanating rays may lose their sparkle and appear dull or limpid. Intellectual and nervous disorders, puberty, menstruation, seem to affect the outer aura. Bagnall says that the aura of a strong person will apparently flow into the aura of a weak person. While some therapeutic "healing" may be possible here, he does not venture to make any bold assertions.

In disease certain dark patches may appear. More telling, however, will be the general shape of the aura.

An aura that falls away suddenly in the neighborhood of the thigh may indicate that a person suffers from nervous complaint.

An outward bulge, away from the spine, is a typical sign of hysteria.

Neurotics usually have a poor outer aura and a dull inner aura.

Physical disturbances seem to affect brightness. Nervous conditions seem to affect the quality of hue.

Bagnall diagnoses pregnancy as follows. The aura becomes broader and deeper over the breasts. There is a widening of the haze in the area immediately below the navel. There is a slight decrease in the clearness of the bluish color, a phenomenon that changes as pregnancy advances.

He feels that medicine and surgery may some day be served through further clinical study. Apparently these emanations that stream from the body have profound significance. The aura of a primitive being is likely to be brownish and coarse in texture. The aura of a new-born babe is slightly greenish. A rather clear blue is a good token of intelligence. Bagnall, after some investigation, believes that this bluish color is as innate to an individual as any other inherited quality—and that it will follow the laws of heredity!

XIV

Body and Brain
Emanations—Today

The human aura: here is one realm in which the mystics of old have won striking victories in modern times. What many skeptics once looked upon as abstruse conjecture, now turns out to be definite fact. Auras were seen and believed in centuries before electromagnetic energy was known to exist. Anyone today who doubts the reality of human emanations (over and above heat, odor and moisture) will himself be in the limbo of the past.

The human body transmits a series of electronic fields. Their emissions can be measured with modern equipment, such as the electroencephalograph (called EEG) which measures brain waves. Energy comes forth from all organs of the body, plus the skin itself. The old mystic and the modern scientist are brought together in the same laboratory.

Let me begin with what is known as Kirlian photography. If the reader is knowledgeable here, please forgive. Articles and books are written these days about "skin talk" in which the body's electrical activity will communicate information about personal thoughts and feeling. There is Kirlian photography which

145

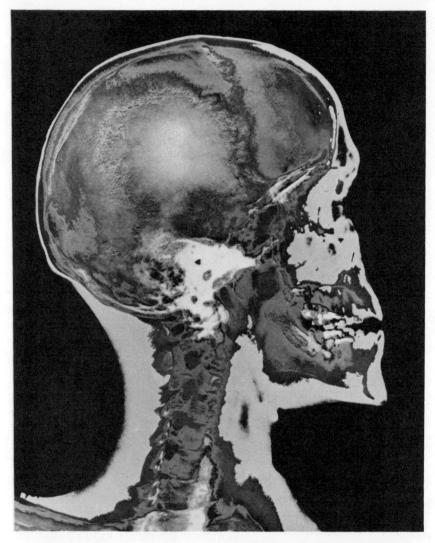

This remarkable photograph is by David K. Hills of Denver, Colorado. He describes it as a "seven-separation color posterization." While it is not a view of the human aura, its brilliant colors in the original--yellow, red, green, blue, violet, magenta--well portray what has long been associated with such emenations.

photographs auras—and biofeedback techniques which reveal emotional and physiological responses to color.

While the mystics spoke of color in glowing and imaginative terms, and while other more sober men wrote of rather obscure procedures, Semyon D. and Valentina Kirlian of Russia, *ca.* 1958, described a method of using high-voltage discharges to photograph "flare patterns" of animate and inanimate things. Fairly successful attempts had been made before, and equally successful attempts have been made since. In what is today known as Kirlian photography the aura has become a matter of tangible and visible record. The world now enters an age of electrodynamics and biodynamics. A good source of reference here is *The Kirlian Aura* by Stanley Krippner and Daniel Rubin.

What is seen? To quote the Kirlians, "It should be noted that when photographing on multilayer color film with disc plates, different parts of a living man's skin are transposed into different colors. For example, the heart region is intensive blue, the forearm is greenish blue, and the thigh is olive. . . . There is reason to assume that during unexpected emotional experiences (e.g., fear and illness) the inherent color in a section changes. It seems to us that these characteristic appearances merit serious study for diagnostic value in medicine for early detection of a disease."

And more from the Kirlians. "Let us stop to consider several electrical occurrences observed on the skin of a living man. In the visual field, on a background of the configuration of the skin, discharge channels with varying characteristics are visible: point, corona, and flares in the form of luminescent clusters. These are of different colors: blue, lavender, and yellow. They may be bright or faded, constant or of varying intensity, periodically flaring up or constantly flaring, motionless or moving. . . . On some sections of skin, points of blue and gold abruptly flare up. Their characteristic feature is a rhythm of flashes and immobility. . . . The color of the clusters may be milky blue, pale lilac, gray, or orange."

Methods of producing Kirlian or radiation field photographs are elaborately described in *The Living Aura* by Kendall Johnson. Ostrander and Schroeder in *Handbook of Psi Discoveries* also describe Kirlian techniques and methods in elaborate detail. Through high voltage discharges—but without lens or camera as such—photographic prints of emissions are recorded. Perhaps it isn't necessary to describe techniques or equipment, for Kirlian Electrophotographic Units are now on the market.

Through electrophotographs of the finger, Johnson reached a number of interesting conclusions. "Rest, relaxation, feeling at ease seemed to be correlated with a wide, bright, smooth corona. . . . Fear or apprehension tended to produce a weak, interrupted corona with a blotch."

Kirlian or radiation field photographs have yet to be made of the body at large. The human aura, from head to foot, described by the mystics of old, and by Kilner and Bagnall in more modern times, has yet to be recorded on any huge photographic film or plate. Perhaps this won't be necessary, for through the study of brain waves and skin responses these days, with excellent equipment, much is learned of man's physical and emotional constitution.

However, to continue with the aura, there are clear indications that shifts and changes in it may indicate, and actually anticipate, physiological and psychological conditions in an individual. In psychosomatic medicine, where environmental conditions may lead to tension, fear, depression, and where these in turn may lead to a number of physiological ailments, a study of the aura may be of great aid in diagnosis. These days, emotional states can be detected in various ways: with the electroencephalograph (which records brain waves), as well as through hormone production, pupil dilation, finger pressure, palmar conductance.

The very existence of the aura may help to explain or at least confirm psychic healing in which certain rare persons can, through "the laying on of hands," offer relief in some conditions of human distress. There are some recognized researchers who believe that through Kirlian photography there is "visible evidence of a flow of energy, or interaction, between human beings and their environments," and that with psychic healers the corona of the healer may flow into the being of the person being treated. This may seem farfetched, but liberal psychosomatic medicine does not totally reject any such "miracles."

Thelma Moss in her book *The Probability of the Impossible* offers good descriptions of Kirlian photography. On the matter of healing she writes, "I do believe that the pictures [Kirlian] show that the energy can travel not only from healer to patient, but from patient to healer." There is also a flow of energy, or interaction between persons and their environment. A healer with a wide corona may transmit energy to a person with a narrow corona.

Electronic devices have been developed to locate acupuncture (hoku) points in the human body. The Russians have one called a "tobiscope," and Kendall Johnson describes one of his own invention. The Russian tobiscope lights up when acupuncture points are touched, and this becomes a mighty useful device for the acupuncture specialist.

Whether or not acupuncture is to be embraced or rejected by the medical profession, one must not forget that the Chinese have recognized it for a few thousand years. Eisenhower's physician, Paul Dudley White, who visited China, wisely wrote, "If it were the world's best technique, we'd all be using it. If it were useless, it would have been dropped thousands of years ago. There's something in it, but it's difficult to say just what." Could it be that acupuncture needs faith and mysticism to support it!

Again as to the aura, corona emanations may not be traceable wholly to skin temperature, galvanic skin response, electrical or magnetic fields, perspiration. There may well be other energy involved, "phenomena that are unpredicted and unexplained by physical theory" (Edgar D. Mitchell in *Psychiatry and Mysticism*). Call it bioplasmic energy or other terms, science no doubt has further and mysterious emanations to comprehend and record.

If the emanations are magnetic, Harold Saxton of Yale maintains that electromagnetic fields within the body are influenced by greater fields throughout the universe—thus confirming the mystic's concept of the little microcosm within the realm of the great macrocosm.

In *Psychiatry and Mysticism* are excellent chapters by Shafica Karagulla of the Royal College of Physicians in Edinburgh and John C. Pierrakos, a practicing psychiatrist and director of the Institute of Bioenergetic Analysis in New York. Dr. Karagulla describes the three auric fields. The first is the vital energy field. This extends about 3 to 5 centimeters beyond the body and has a bluish haze. The second field, which has a changing pattern of colors, reveals a person's emotions. The third field is the mental one which "exhibits the quality of the mind and thinking of the individual." There is a fourth integrating field.

These fields can be used for diagnostic purposes, according to

Dr. Karagulla. The energy vortex at the throat has a pale blue or violet color in a healthy person. Red or orange reveals problems in the thyroid which might be detected in advance.

Some gifted doctors have been known to see auras in their patients and to diagnose from them, usually without making any reference whatsoever to the insight.

Dr. Pierrakos also describes the aura and tells of equipment used to measure it. He speaks of three layers or fields. "The principle movement of the three layers can be described as a wave moving away from the body. . . . I consider the field to be primarily an expression of all aspects of man—physical, emotional, mental, and spiritual." These are statements of a psychiatrist, not a mystic! He further wrote, "Human beings seem to swim in a sea of fluid, tinged rhythmically with brilliant colors which constantly change hues, shimmer, and vibrate. In truth, to be alive is to be colorful and vibrant."

He noted various changes in illness. Fear caused a dulling effect. Schizophrenic patients showed severe disturbances.

Let this chapter now proceed with references to human skin and the human brain. Numerous articles and at least one book have been written about "skin talk." (The book is *Touching: The Human Significance of the Skin,* by Ashley Montagu.) Virtually everyone has experienced pink blush, clammy hands, wet armpits. With the lie detector (polygraph), skin conductance is readily noted and charted. What happens is that electrical impulses are recorded which surprisingly give away a person's feelings—not invariably, but generally. The machine can communicate information about a person's emotions. Jung experimented with it and noted that the skin's electrical activity could even be affected by word associations.

Further, "The skin sees in technicolor," writes Barbara B. Brown in her remarkable book *New Mind, New Body.* The skin could discriminate among colors. "The skin also is a good color detector and seems to reflect the way in which brain neurons process color information. Experiments demonstrating body reactions to color support the common belief that colors induce emotional states which are specific to different hues." Perhaps the day may come when the procedure could be reversed—the reaction of the skin in different emotional states could light up different colors. When different colors were projected on a screen, the polygraph showed stronger response to red than to green—and greater response to violet than to green. The information recorded evidently was picked up by the brain through the eye and then expressed electrically by the skin. Auras obviously are involved here.

Regarding brain waves, let me disgress a bit. Robert Ornstein and Roger Sperry have developed a theory that the two hemispheres of the brain have different functions. Both men have been concerned with biofeedback techniques and with brain wave responses.

In brief, the left hemisphere of the brain is good at logic, while the right hemisphere is more intuitive. Lawyers were likely to have more active left hemispheres, while artists had more active right hemispheres.

From the polygraph, which measures skin response, to the electroencephalograph (EEG), which measures brain waves, the aura still shines. Just about all parts of the human body generate electrical current. This is especially true of the brain. Here enough electrical energy can be developed, which, properly amplified, can turn lights off and on (and run toy electric trains). So-called biofeedback is becoming of great popular appeal. There is a Bio-Feedback Research Society, and hundreds of researchers and research reports have been devoted to the phenomenon. The Edmund Scientific Company, which makes Kirlian photographic equipment, also has available biofeedback monitors and alpha wave sensors (1976) ranging in price from $19.95 to $299.95 and over. What was once a scientific development has unfortunately become a pseudo-scientific plaything. A GSR Monitor is also made to check the reactions of plants to light, touch, music, the human voice, smoke, etc.

Through the control of alpha (and other) waves by an individual, body reactions can be regulated from the inside-out, so to speak. Control of alpha waves, as an aid to meditation, is showing promise in psychomatic medicine of relieving such problems as high blood pressure, insomnia, asthma and in the rehabilitation of drug users. It can also cope with psychological fears, tensions and frustrations.

Now as to color, Barbara Brown set forth to determine "Whether feelings about color modify brain waves or whether brain waves are first affected by colors and the feelings developed later." Brain wave activity was recorded when different colors were exposed. Here are two of her conclusions.

"The overlap between the associations between color and feeling states and the associations between color and brain waves . . . suggests the possibility that subjective activity relating to colors may originate from the same underlying neuronal processes as do the brain waves.

"I tend to favor the concept that the brain cell, neuronal, response to color came first, since in my studies and those of others the brain electrical response to red is one of alerting or arousal, where the brain electrical response to blue is one of relaxation. This happens in animals as well as man."

Biofeedback techniques have as of this writing lost much of their charm. Many practitioners, clinical groups, sectional and regional meetings have been dissolved. Yet biofeedback has become an affair of great interest to diagnostic and therapeutic medicine, and it no doubt will be continually investigated into the future. In one interesting suggestion of Barbara Brown, human anxiety states (such as related to unemployment) might be treated as follows. A series of pictures related to a person's anxiety, would be projected on a screen. A row of small, colored lights would be placed along the edge of the screen and activated by brain wave or muscle activity. A person might then become aware of what specific situations distress him and learn to control or change his responses.

So the aura, skin response, brain response—and also perhaps heart and respiration, blood pressure—seem to be involved with color through electrical impulses. The ancient mystic or shaman healer, the faith healer, the modern psychiatrist and clinical psychologist all have been and should be concerned with the rainbow that surrounds all beings. Fable is being supported by fact. The world is colorful, inside and out.

XV

Meditation vs. Sensory Deprivation

A good part of this chapter has been drawn from a previous book of mine, *Color and Human Response*. Having a strong interest in mysticism as a young man, I gave myself to meditation as practiced by occultists and yogis. I now confess to failure for the most part. Meditation these days seems to appeal largely to disturbed souls in search of peace within themselves. Perhaps the effort failed with me because I had no particular interest in peace of mind or peace of soul. To stimulate alpha waves through utter relaxation somehow ran contrary to my inner disposition. I knew from the biographies of great men that worry, discontent, anxiety, depression often led to high accomplishment. None of these scourges bothered me much. I further knew that total euphoria could be a form of insanity.

If meditation could lead to peace, it also could lead to boredom, and this was paradoxical.

Color is involved here for reasons to be explained. Where monotony may be forced upon a person, an adverse condition of sensory deprivation may follow. This might apply to anyone leading a dreary life, to old people in retirement homes, to prisoners,

THE FOOL .

shipwrecked sailors, persons confined to bed for heart attacks or broken bones. Sensory deprivation, a topic of national conferences, books and monographs, does inimical things to body and mind.

Maybe if men could learn to meditate, to control their physiological functions, their minds and emotions, all would be well. But only temporarily, of course. *It is a strictly normal and natural condition for all the senses to be stimulated continually, even if moderately. A condition of absolute peace is unnatural.* As a British psychologist put it, "Thus we must conclude that normal consciousness, perception and thought can be maintained only in a constantly changing environment. When there is no change, a state of 'sensory deprivation' occurs; the capacity of adults to concentrate deteriorates, attention fluctuates and lapses, and normal perception fades. In infants who have not developed a full understanding of their environment, the whole personality may be affected, and readjustment to a normal environment may be difficult." (M. D. Vernon.)

It could be that meditation, for some at least, would be upsetting rather than consoling.

Mysticism has to do with sensory deprivation because of the strange things that happen during prolonged isolation or repose. First of all, brainwashing of prisoners has included lack of sleep, hard labor, lack of privacy, heckling. The Russians relied a great deal on isolation and monotony. In America solitary confinement has been extreme punishment (sadism excluded). Religious sects have resorted to "shunning" and to the sending of dissenters and sinners to "Coventry."

Left alone, men have illusions and hallucinations. Their perceptions are distorted and their intelligence deteriorates. There is great susceptibility to influence. If the reader thinks that absolute peace, with or without meditation, is conducive to creative thinking, let him be warned: he may find himself lost in a dull or perhaps ominous stupor!

Sensory deprivation may lead to effects that are quite similar to those that follow the taking of hallucinogenic drugs such as LSD. Forms may seem distorted, colors changed in saturation, a sense of time confused and clear thought jumbled. Thus if meditation is supposed to assure proverbial peace and quiet, it may also excite distressing anxiety.

This strange photograph of a modern discotheque shows a 7,000-pound "mothership" being lowered from above, lights flashing and sounds blaring. There seems to be a psychological and psychic relationship between the hallucinations that follow sensory deprivation and the effects of extreme sensory stimulation. (United Press International Photo.)

If there is danger in being alone, too much "togetherness" may as well cause trouble. In small groups of people, some persons will seek privacy and withdrawal. Confinement in spaceships, submarines, institutions, dormatories will often pit friend against friend. Admiral Byrd in his book, *Alone,* writes: "Even at Little America I knew of bunkmates who quit speaking because each suspected the other of inching his gear into the other's allotted space; and I knew of one who could not eat unless he could find a place in the mess hall out of sight of the Fletcherist who solemnly chewed his food twenty-eight times before swallowing. In a polar camp little things like that have the power to drive even disciplined men to the edge of insanity. During my first winter at Little America I walked for hours with a man who was on the verge of murder or suicide over imaginary persecutions by another man who had been his devoted friend. For there is no escape anywhere. You are hemmed in on every side by your own inadequacies and the crowding pressures of your associates. The ones who survive with a measure of happiness are those who can live profoundly off their intellectual resources."

Note the last sentence. If a person would seek peace and happiness in meditation—which might well lead to sensory deprivation—he might be better advised to develop his "intellectual resources."

Meditation is not for everyone. Yet mind-training courses have been given broadly to thousands of hopeful mortals, often with excellent results. If a person, through anxiety or other distress, finds comfort and relief in meditation, this is all to the good. Yet I confess to a certain skepticism and prejudice. Some people who take mind-training courses become neurotic. There is danger in burrowing too deeply into one's psyche. There may be quite the opposite of "the Kingdom of Heaven" within. Gary E. Schwartz writes in *Psychiatry and Mysticism,* "The nervous system needs reasonably intense and varied external stimulation, and there is no evolutionary, ethological, or biological precedent for massive and prolonged meditation."

Mind-training, mind-control, biofeedback sometimes rely on hypnosis, too, and this, frankly, scares me. Some who have posed as mystics or spiritual leaders have used hypnosis as a technique. If phenomenal results have been achieved at times, so also has backlash caused reverse and adverse effects.

Not to disparage meditation entirely, however, it can have beneficial effects. Through the control of alpha and theta waves by voluntary concentration (and as recorded by professional biofeedback instruments), various favorable therapeutic results may follow. Through lessened anxiety and tension, high blood pressure (hypertension) may be relieved if not cured. There may be applications for those troubled by depression, insomnia, addiction to alcohol and drugs. Perhaps this isn't mysticism, but at least it involves phenomena none too clearly understood by the fact-minded scientist.

To return to the mystic, consider the meditation rituals of the Buddhist. Yellow was worn in the ordination of the Buddhist priest. "In compassion for me, lord, give me these yellow robes and let me be ordained." Yoga practices generally refer to certain hues. Among the forty subjects of meditation, designed to establish communion between the holy one and the infinite, were the dark blue kasina, the yellow kasina, the blood red kasina, the white kasina, a purple corpse. In contemplation the religious one was to gaze upon unprepared earth, either a plowed field or a threshing floor. In the earth kasina careful instructions were presented. "The colors dark blue, yellow, blood red and white are imperfections in this kasina. Therefore, in practicing this kasina, one must avoid clay of any one of these colors, and use light red clay, such as is found in the bed of the Ganges."

Another set of instructions as to what a meditating Buddhist should think about is found in the *Tantrik Texts*. Here the ritual of color is most important.

"Imagine on the letter A a lunar disk, red and white, about the size of the half of a pea, inside one's heart. Upon the lunar disk imagine a light-point about the size of a mustard seed which is the concentrated form of one's mind. Fix the mind on that and regulate the breath gently. . . .

"Imagine within the two pupils of the eyes, that there are two very fine bright white points, one in each eye. Close the eyes and imagine in your mind that the points are there. . . .

"After this, transfer the imagination to the ears. Imagine two blue points or dots upon two lunar disks the size of a half-pea inside each ear and meditate upon them, in a place free from noise. . . .

"Then transfer the imagination to the nose. Imagine a yellow point on a lunar disk in the cavity of each nostril in a place free from any odor, and concentrate your mind on that. . . .

"Next transfer the imagination to the tongue. Imagine a red point on a lunar disk at the root of the tongue, and meditate on it without tasting any flavor. . . .

"Then transfer your imagination to the body. Either at the root of the secret parts, or on your forehead, imagine a green point on a lunar disk, and fix your mind on it without touching anything. . . .

"Then after that, transfer the imagination to the mind, which moves everywhere. Imagine a very small pink point on the top of that already imagined as being within the heart. . . .

"Then imagine that the chief passion—infatuation—which accompanies all other evil passions, is concentrated in it. Think that it is absorbed into a blue point. Fix the mind on that. . . .

"When one has attained firmness in that, sink the blue point into the pink point, and that into the white and red point below it. Then the last sinks into the moon-disk; which in its turn is dissolved or disappears in the sky like a cloud. Then there remains only emptiness, in which the mind is to be kept at a level."

IX

THE HERMIT.

XVI

Of LSD, Eidetic Imagery and Eyeless Sight

The mystic has won further victories beyond public acknowledgement of the human aura. The process of color vision remains largely unknown to science. Indeed, the study of vision has shifted from optics to physiology to neurology. Today it is the brain that is given major attention, and here the psyche also dwells.

Such phenomena as afterimages, dreams, visions, hallucinations are neural in character—they are in the brain, not in the eye. The mystic has been saying this right along, and now the scientist must pay heed.

In the '60s a drug cult rose in America on the simple foundation of a drop of *lysergic acid diethylamide* (LSD) on a lump of sugar. Suddenly across the nation countless persons, mostly young, swallowed the lump of sugar and took celestial trips, one of the most notable features of which was an explosion of brilliant, flowing and flashing color, the likes of which had never been witnessed on earth. In effect, the amazing discovery was made that a fantastic world of color existed within the human psyche. It

161

lay buried as if in a golden cask, and a drop of LSD opened it up and let its magic burst forth. Here the process of vision was reversed—it came from the inside out, not from the outside in.

How was science to explain this? Never mind. While youths by the thousand lay on bare or carpeted floors and took acid trips— bum ones or grand ones—the medical profession diligently sought applications of the wonder drug. It had possibilities in some mental cases. It could be used to create states of euphoria in terminal cases. It could wipe out fear of death. It was, in effect, mind-expanding. It was inexpensive and amazingly potent: an eyedropper full of LSD was enough for 5,000 trips. Threats were made to put a few ounces in public water supplies and send masses of citizens out into the psychic stratospheres.

Hallucinogenic drugs had been known for centuries in hashish, opium, peyote, mescal. Derived from cactus, peyote was taken by the American Indian as part of religious ritual. The LSD cult in America during the '60s also frequently used it for religious purposes—to achieve harmony with all that was infinite.

How to describe the effects of LSD? Aldous Huxley wrote, "Mescaline raises all colors to a higher power and makes the percipient aware of innumerable fine shades of difference, to which, at ordinary times, he is completely blind." Heinrich Klüver declared, "It is impossible to find words to describe mescal colors." Visions often have an Oriental quality, like Oriental rugs come to life, but with colors of fabulous intensity.

One outstanding authority on LSD is Stanislav Grof. He has been chief of psychiatric research at the Maryland Psychiatric Research Center in Baltimore and assistant professor of psychiatry at Johns Hopkins University. Dr. Grof has done experimental work with LSD for over 15 years and has conducted over 2,000 psychedelic sessions. In *Psychiatry and Mysticism* (edited by Stanley R. Dean), he devotes a remarkable chapter to describe many of his observations. LSD trips can be down as well as up. There can, on the one hand, be feelings of cosmic unity, holiness, peace, bliss, and on the other hand extreme terror.

Grof offers many fascinating references to the experiences of different individuals.

There can be cosmic engulfment, feelings of evil, persecution, with visions of dragons, pythons, octopus: "A cosmic maelstrom sucking the subject and his world relentlessly to the center."

The LSD cults of the late sixties and seventies, in experiments with hallucinogenic drugs, discovered a fantastic world of brilliant and dynamic color within the human psyche. If color sensation came from an exterior world, a far more ecstatic experience came from an inner one. (United Press International Photo.)

There can be concepts of hell, unbearable suffering, war, epidemic, catastrophy.

There can be death and rebirth, the release of great energy, with visions of explosions, volcanoes, atom bombs.

There can be total annihilation, ego death. There can also be an overwhelming feeling of love. "The universe is perceived as indescribably beautiful." There can be "Visions of radiant sources of light experienced as divine, of a heavenly blue color, of a rainbow spectrum, of peacock feathers."

To bear out Jung's theory of the collective unconscious, some takers of LSD may witness their own birth and delivery from their mother's womb. There can be echoes of Greek mythology, Biblical stories, pagan ceremonies. There can be ancestral throwbacks in which a person relives the experiences of his progenitors.

There can be face-to-face meetings with the deities of old—Isis, Mazda, Apollo, Jehovah, Christ. Writes Grof, "The encounter with these deities is usually accompanied by very powerful emotions, ranging from metaphysical horror to ecstatic rapture."

Grof's interest has been to use LSD to treat various emotional disorders, schizophrenia, sexual deviation, alcoholism, drug addiction. His sessions, however, have also included scientists, philosophers, artists, educators.

The taking of LSD has led to new art forms. In addition to brilliant colors, visions often reveal wavy lines, mosaics, flowers, animals, geometric patterns, jewels, gratings, lattice, honeycombs, fretwork, all of which tend to be animate. Artists have attempted to put these visions on canvas.

Out of the LSD cult came the discothéque of the late '60s. Reversing the procedure of psychochemical ingestion, psychedelic discotheques using flashing lights, flowing colors, fluid designs and patterns, roaring sounds, attempted with fair success in blanking out the real world for one of psychic and nightmarish fancy—without the taking of drugs. Flashing lights have been found to induce seizures in epilepsy, while pulsating, stroboscopic flashes may be hypnotic, produce headaches, nausea and minor forms of a nervous breakdown.

This all relates to mysticism, for it has demonstrated in a clear way psychic experiences of individual inner worlds. Involved with eidetic imagery (to be discussed), with the effects of sensory deprivation, a world inside the brain has been known among mystics since the beginning of time. Religious ecstasy has led to manifestations of bleeding statues, the startling appearance of gods and apparitions, the dead come to life. Not all of this has been "imagination," for where visions have been encountered (among alcoholics, for example), eye movements have been noted and recorded by laboratory technicians. The visions are definitely there because the brain puts them there—right out in front.

Subjective color effects exist abundantly in man the microcosm, colors that register in his brain without any colors actually being before his eyes. Centuries ago Aristotle noted a "flight of colors" upon looking into the sun. He wrote, "If after having looked at the sun or some other bright object, we close the eyes, then, if we watch carefully, it appears on a right line with the direction of vision, at first with its own color, then it changes to crimson, next to purple, until it becomes black and disappears."

Goethe saw the sequence of brightness first, then yellow, purple, and blue. Sun-gazing is a dangerous pastime. With less risk a person may gaze at a frosted electric light bulb or a strongly illuminated piece of white paper. If the stimulus is of high intensity, the sequence may begin at green and proceed through blue, green, into black. Though these hues have no external existence they are quite real to the senses and will move with the eyes, have form and be localized in space.

LSD, of course, heightens this all the more.

In recent years the study of mental imagery has led to the discovery of numerous and astonishing phenomena. A notable investigator in this field has been E. R. Jaensch. The images experienced by humans fall into three types—memory-images, afterimages, eidetic images. The first of these is the product of mind and imagination, having the quality of an idea or thought. The afterimage is more literal. It is actually seen and may have shape, design, dimension, precise hue. Its size will vary as the eye gazes at near or far surfaces. Generally it is a complementary image, white being seen where black was originally, red being replaced by green, and so on.

The third type, the eidetic image, is the most remarkable of all. Jaensch writes: "Eidetic images are phenomena that take up an intermediate position between sensations and images. Like ordinary physiological afterimages, they are always *seen* in the literal sense. They have this property of necessity under all conditions and share it with sensations."

Eidetic imagery is the gift of childhood, youth, the insane, the mystically inspired. While seemingly akin to the supernatural, it is nonetheless a sensory reality. The child playing with his toys may be able to project living pictures of them in his mind. These may not be mere products of the imagination. They may be far more tangible, with dimension, color, movement in their make-up. They are "lantern-slides" of the eye and brain, projected into definite, localized space. They are images as real as projected lantern-slides.

People in an hysterical state due to drugs or mental aberrations may find themselves attacked by ghoulish adversaries. Some have been known to run for their lives and even leap from windows. To some in the grip of delirium tremens, rats have crept out of walls and wires have projected from fingertips.

The phenomenon for the most part was given little attention up to recent years. Because it vanishes with age and is likely to disappear at puberty, the adult mind, capable of dealing with it, relegates it to the fervid period of childhood. Nevertheless images are seen. Pictures stand before the eyes and details are distinguished in them which may be counted and identified in hue.

What mystics have declared, and what the mentally troubled have described, all too often have been passed aside as the delusions of persons "out of their minds." According to Jaensch, however, eidetic images are subject to the same laws as other sensations and perceptions. They are, "in truth, merely the most obvious sign of the structure of personality normal to youth." Through them science might find plausible explanations for the reports of saints that walk out of pictures, of weird creatures, ghouls and demons seen by human eyes. Because eidetic images are real sensations, ghouls and demons may also be real. And instead of singing incantations and prescribing insanity tests, it might be better to treat the confessed observer as a sane human with a mental acuteness perhaps beyond the common stamp.

For most persons there is an admitted gap between sensation and imagery. This viewpoint is generally a dodge to support the triteness that reality and imagination are distinctly different. Jaensch says, "Some people have peculiar 'intermediate experiences' between sensations and images." They are true eidetics whose responses are quite frank and spontaneous. To them sensation and imagination may go hand in hand and be closely united in some literal and graphic visual experience.

To discover this eidetic personality Jaensch has outlined three test procedures. Although he is aware of the phenomenon in small children he prefers youngsters of ten years or more, because they are better able to comprehend what the psychologist is trying to find out and to express themselves.

First, the individual (or group of individuals) is cautioned that literal images and not memory-pictures are to be recorded. To reveal the character of the true eidetic image, simple experiments are made with afterimages. A gray background is set up (about 14 per cent white and 86 per cent black by color-wheel measurement). A square of red paper is visually concentrated upon for 20 seconds. The individual then sees a green area of similar size. He is told that this is a *real* experience and has a physiological basis. It is not in the least mystic or occult.

Repeating the experiment, but shortening the exposition time of the color sample, individuals are found who continue to see afterimages, some of them with prolonged duration. To a few, this afterimage will no longer be the complement of the sample (a green afterimage for red), but an image that is the *same hue* as the sample. Here the eidetic faculty is of relatively high degree.

Second, the eidetics, now located, are shown a fairly complicated silhouette picture having numerous details and being slightly larger than a postcard. This is fixated for 15 seconds. The average person will see a somewhat blurred image, having bright and dark areas that are complementary to the original (and more like a normal afterimage). The eidetic, however, will see the whole picture or a greater part of it, and in colors that correspond to the original!

Third, the above experiments are continued with other pictures having an interest to attract the child. The fixation period is shortened still more. The true eidetic is revealed, and the pictures continue to live for him, projected before his eyes as literal things and experiences!

Eidetic images are filmy like afterimages. Although the original objects which prompt them may be of textured hues, the eidetic image is more like light. It is, as mentioned, a positive rather than a negative "picture." In some instances it may be tri-dimensional.

Jaensch reports that the eidetic image is easier to recall than the memory-image.

He also found that treatments with calcium caused the eidetic disposition to be *weaker*. The image seen under this circumstance was likely to be complementary in hue and brightness to the original. Conversely, treatments with potassium occasionally made a latent type active and considerably heightened the eidetic disposition.

To describe one of these images, one investigator of the phenomenon tells of the reactions of a Professor Schilder. After gazing at a colored picture representing boys at play, Schilder "first sees a red cap and a drum, the drumstick moving rapidly at considerable distance from the drum; four indistinct faces and something green. Concentrating to get an eidetic image with the characteristics of the real picture, the four figures become distinct and a green apron becomes clearly visible below the row of the boys. The observer feels that there must be something to the left: a wooden sabre appears in the field to the left. There is also a boy marching above the drum. His legs move frantically, and the trumpet he blows is moving back and forth."

The phenomenon of eidetic imagery has all the charm of magic and clairvoyance. In a more practical light, however, it may serve useful ends. Jaensch writes, "The eidetic investigators have already shown that the closest resemblance to the mind of the child is not the mental structure of the logician, but that of the artist." In education, the forcing of an adult viewpoint, mind and manner upon the child suppresses the eidetic personality and consequently may stand in the way of creative and natural expression. "For example, an eidetic child may, without special effort, reproduce symbols taken from the Phoenician alphabet, Hebrew words, etc. Or a person with a strong eidetic imagery may look at a number of printed words for a while and then go to the dark room and revive the text eidetically. It is possible to photograph the eye-movements occurring during the reading of the eidetic text."

Some authorities have striven to relate eidetic imagery to personality. Introverts are said to show a tendency to see meaningful, interrelated wholes. Extroverts tend to have reactions that are more objective and analytical in character.

In psychiatry the eidetic image has been termed an "undertone of psychosis." No doubt the subject has psychiatric importance. It may, for example, have bearing on theories of hallucinations. It may also throw new light on the mysteries of human perception and on the dynamics of life in general. The mystic, so familiar with visions, has frequently been sent to Coventry by the scientist. He may find himself invited back into the laboratory.

To end this chapter, let me tell of what has been called Eyeless Sight. In 1924 the French author, Jules Romains (he wrote numerous novels and plays), published a book with the title mentioned. While he never did enlist the support of the French Academy of Science, the success of his experiments was affirmed by many famous scientists and scholars, among them Anatole France, who stoutly defended his theories.

According to the Frenchman the skin of man was sensitive to light (a fact that certainly is true among certain lower forms of life). This he called paroptic perception. Using specially designed screens so that light would reach various parts of the body—but not the eyes—he stimulated this paroptic perception to action. I quote from his book: "For example, if the hands are bare, the sleeves lifted to the elbows, the forehead clear, the chest uncovered, the subject reads easily at a normal speed, a page of a novel or an article in a newspaper, printed in ordinary print."

Romains declared the hands to be most sensitive, then the neck and throat, cheeks, forehead, chest, back of neck, arms, thighs, ec. Elemental images were formed in the tactile nerves which "saw" color as well as form. "Our experiments place beyond doubt the existence in man of a *paroptic function,* that is, a function of visual perception of exterior objects (color and form), without the intervention of the ordinary mechanism of vision through the eyes." He contended that any intelligent person might be able to read the titles of a newspaper while blindfolded. And, "Under normal illumination the qualitative perception of colors is perfect." One might even "smell" colors through one's nose. "Perception of colors by the nasal mucosa is not of an olfactory order; that is, it does not consist in a recognition of *odors* belonging to the coloring substances. It is a perception specifically optical."

Not much happened for some time after Romains, for the world in which he lived was an incredulous one that demanded facts more solid than the ones presented. Then about 40 years later a fabulous lady (then others) was found who could read and distinguish colors with the tips of her fingers. This revived fascination with a phenomenon and fad that gained international publicity.

An excellent account of modern eyeless sight is given in the Ostrander and Schroeder book, *Psychic Discoveries Behind the Iron Curtain*. A Russian girl, Rosa Kuleshova, could see with her fingers! Doubting doctors witnessed her ability to read type and name colors "as if she'd grown a second set of eyes in her fingertips."

Rosa was taken to Moscow where she continued to perform wonders under close scrutiny. She still could "see" red, green, blue when the colored sheets were covered with tracing paper, cellophane or glass. The great Russian Biophysics Institute of the Academy of Sciences was bewildered but had to admit Rosa's "dermo-optics." *Life* magazine sent a reporter to Moscow and later ran a feature, illustrated story (June 12, 1964).

Then others appeared who had the same mystical ability, including a woman from Michigan. It seemed that some colors were sticky, some smooth, some rough. "Light blue is smoothest. You feel yellow as very slippery, but not quite as smooth. Red, green, and dark blue are sticky. You feel green as stickier than red, but not as coarse. Navy blue comes over as the stickiest, but yet harder than red and green. Orange is hard, very rough, and causes a braking feeling. Violet gives a greater braking effect that seems to slow the hand and feels even rougher."

There is a relationship here to eidetic imagery, for eyeless sight seemed to be a natural endowment. "It is most noticeable in children from the ages of seven to twelve years."

Could the blind be trained to see and distinguish colors with fingers, elbow, tongue, nose?

Since Rosa Kuleshova, the Russians have further investigated skin sight in hopes that the blind could be given at least some "visual" perception, even if weak. A few have been so trained. Perhaps as long as the true organ of perception is in the brain, not in the eye, clues from the body, the skin, are what the blind can use to "see" the world and its spectral hues. "If certain critical objects like doorknobs, faucets, telephones, handles on pots, dishes, particularly movable objects were colored, say, yellow in a room brilliantly lit with yellow bulbs, the blind might actually be able to see with their skin almost as easily as we locate a coffeepot with our eyes."

Certainly, as has been discussed regarding the human aura, if the skin definitely responds to colors and relates them to different emotional states—then why could not literal, photographic images be sensed as well!

Quite the opposite of eyeless sight is a phenomenon that has been called psychic photography or thoughtography. While spiritualistic photographs have been exhibited in the past (ghostly images hovering about the heads of living mortals) much of this has aroused suspicion. Whether or not spirits can materialize enough to have their pictures taken, reference can be made to the well-documented case of Ted Serios of Chicago and Denver. Ted Serios was a poorly educated bellhop in Chicago in the early '40s. He was temperamental, perhaps a bit psychopathic, and he had a drinking problem.

Ted Serios could stare into a Polaroid camera and out would come (at times) vague photographs, less of people, than of things such as places, structures, the Eiffel Tower, Taj Mahal, White House. Dr. Jule Eisenbud, a psychiatrist and fellow of the American Psychiatric Association, took Ted Serios under his wing, so to speak, moved him to Denver and for two years submitted the man to a series of experiments which were, in time, witnessed by dozens of friends, scientists, photographers, magicians. The result was an illustrated book of 368 pages (see Bibliography).

A skeptical person might bring his own Polaroid camera, his own film, hold the device himself and even trip the shutter, and out would come (not always, unfortunately) phantom prints of windmills, ships, automobiles, the tower of Westminster Abbey or a double-deck English bus.

Ted Serios could not explain his talent, nor did he have any interest in attempting to do so. He said that the gift would pass, and after a while it did. In his fascinating book, Jule Eisenbud comments, "Dr. Hans Berger, the discoverer of brain waves, granted the possible reality of telepathic communication but did not believe that whatever type of brain wave 'radiation' was measured by the EEG could account for them."

Bibliography

Note. Over many years, scores of books, publications and other writings have been consulted in the preparation of this present work. Some of these references, unfortunately, have not always been identified, and some may have been misplaced. In any event, the more important sources are given below for those who may wish to pursue further the intriguing subjects involved.

Achad, Fraten (C. Stansfeld Jones), Q. B. L., *The Bride's Reception,* (Printed by the Author), Chicago, 1922.

Aston, W. G., *Shinto, the Way of the Gods,* Longmans, Green, and Co., London, 1905.

Ayscough, Florence, *Symbolism of the Forbidden City, Peking,* Journal of the North-China Branch of the Royal Asiatic Society, Vol. LXI, 1930.

Babbitt, Edwin D., *The Principles of Light and Color* (1878), edited and annotated by Faber Birren, Citadel Press, Secaucus, N. J., 1978.

Bagnall, Oscar, *The Origin and Properties of the Human Aura,* E. P. Dutton & Co., New York, 1937.

Benet, Stephen Vincent, *The Devil and Daniel Webster,* Farrar, New York, 1937.

173

Birren, Faber, *The Story of Color,* Crimson Press, Westport, Connecticut, 1941.

Birren, Faber, *Color Psychology and Color Therapy,* Citadel Press, Secaucus, N. J., 1978.

Birren, Faber, *Color—A Survey in Words and Pictures,* Citadel Press, Secaucus, N. J., 1984.

Birren, Faber, *Color in Your World,* Collier Books, New York, 1961, 1978.

Birren, Faber, *Light, Color and Environment,* Van Nostrand Reinhold Co., New York, 1982.

Birren, Faber, *Color and Human Response,* Van Nostrand Reinhold Co., New York, 1978.

Blum, Harold Francis, *Photodynamic Action and Diseases Caused by Light,* Reinhold Publishing Corp., 1941.

Brown, Barbara B., *New Mind, New Body,* Harper & Row, New York, 1974.

Budge, E. A. Wallis, *Amulets and Superstitions,* Oxford University Press, London, 1930.

Budge, E. A. Wallis, *The Book of the Dead,* University Books, New Hyde Park, New York, 1960.

Burton, Sir Richard, *The Arabian Nights,* Modern Library, Random House, New York, 1920.

Byrd, R. E., *Alone,* Putnam, New York, 1938.

Catholic Encyclopedia, The Universal Knowledge Foundation, New York, 1914.

Cayce, Edgar, *Auras,* A. R. E. Press, Virginia Beach, Virginia, 1945.

Celsus on Medicine, C. Cox, London, 1831.

Churchward, Albert, *The Signs and Symbols of Primordial Man,* Swan Sonnenschein & Co., London, 1910.

Cockerell, C. R., *The Temples of Jupiter Pan-Hellenius and Apollo Epicurius,* John Weale, London, 1860.

Cohen, David, "Magnetic Fields of the Human Body," *Physics Today,* August, 1975.

Corlett, William Thomas, *The Medicine Man of the American Indian,* Charles C. Thomas, Springfield, Illinois, 1935.

Darwin, Charles, *The Descent of Man* (reprint of second edition, 1874), A. L. Purt Co., New York.

Da Vinci, Leonardo, *A Treatise on Painting,* George Bell & Sons, London, 1877.

Dean, Stanley R., editor, *Psychiatry and Mysticism,* Nelson-Hall, Chicago, 1975.

De Givry, Grillot, *Witchcraft, Magic and Alchemy,* George G. Harrap & Co., Ltd., London, 1931.

Dictionary of the Bible, (Edited by William Smith and J. M. Fuller),

John Murray, London, 1893.

Dictionary of Christian Antiquities, (Edited by William Smith and Samuel Cheetham), Little, Brown, and Company, Boston, 1875.

Duggar, Benjamin M., editor, *Biological Effects of Radiation,* McGraw-Hill Book Co., New York, 1936.

Dutt, Nripendra Kumar, *Origin and Growth of Caste in India,* Kegan Paul, Trench, Trubner & Co., London, 1931.

Eisenbud, Jule, *The World of Ted Serios,* William Morrow & Co., New York, 1967.

Ellinger, E. F., *The Biological Fundamentals of Radiation Therapy,* American Elsevier Publishing Co., New York, 1941.

Ellinger, E. F., *Medical Radiation Biology,* Charles C. Thomas, Springfield, Illinois, 1957.

Fergusson, James, *A History of Architecture in All Countries,* John Murray, London, 1893.

Figulus, Benedictus, *A Golden and Blessed Casket of Nature's Marvels,* James Elliott and Co., London, 1893.

Fox, William Sherwood, *The Mythology of all Races,* edited by Louis Herbert Gray, Marshall Jones Co., Boston, 1916.

Frazer, J. G., *The Golden Bough,* Macmillan, London, 1911.

Goethe, Johann Wolfgang von, *Theory of Colours (Farbenlehre),* translated by Charles Lock Eastlake, John Murray, London, 1840.

Goldstein, Kurt, *The Organism,* American Book Co., New York, 1939.

Gregory, R. L., *Eye and Brain,* World University Library, New York, 1967.

Gregory, R. L., *The Intelligent Eye,* McGraw-Hill Book Co., New York, 1970.

Gruner, O. Cameron, *A Treatise on the Canon of Medicine of Avicenna,* Luzac & Co., London, 1930.

Haggard, Howard W., *Devils, Drugs and Doctors,* Harper & Bros., New York, 1929.

Hall, Manly P., *An Encyclopedic Outline of Masonic, Hermetic, Qabbalistic and Rosicrucian Symbolic Philosophy,* H. S. Crocker Co., San Francisco, 1928.

Hartmann, Franz, *Cosmology,* Occult Publishing Co., Boston, 1888.

Hartmann, Franz, *Magic, White and Black,* Metaphysical Publishing Co., New York, 1890.

Heckewelder, Rev. John, *Diary,* Ohio State Archaeological and Historical Quarterly, Vol. 61, No. 3, July, 1952.

Hill, Justina, *Germs and Man,* G. D. Putnam's Sons, New York, 1940.

Hulme, F. Edward, *Symbolism in Christian Art,* Macmillan & Co., New York, 1891.

Huxley, Aldous, *The Doors of Perception,* Harper & Row, New York, 1963.

Jaensch, E. R., *Eidetic Imagery*, Kegan Paul, Trench, Trubner & Co., London, 1930.

Jayne, Walter Addison, *The Healing Gods of Ancient Civilizations*, Yale University Press, New Haven, 1925.

Jewish Encyclopedia, Funk and Wagnalls Company, New York, 1903.

Johnson, Kendall, *The Living Aura*, Hawthorne Books, New York, 1975.

Josephus, *Collected Works, The Antiquities of the Jews*, David McKay, Philadelphia, 1896.

Jung, Carl, *The Integration of the Personality*, Farrar & Rinehart, New York, 1939.

Jung, Carl, *Psychology and Alchemy*, Pantheon Books, Bollingen Series XX, New York, 1953.

Kilner, Walter J., *The Human Atmosphere*, Rebman Co., New York, 1911.

Klüver, Heinrich, *Mescal and Mechanisms of Hallucinations*, University of Chicago Press, Chicago, 1966.

Knight, Richard Payne, *The Symbolical Language of Ancient Art and Mythology*, J. W. Bouton, New York, 1876.

Koran of Mohammed, translated by George Sale, Regan Publishing Corp., Chicago, 1921.

Krippner, Stanley and Daniel Rubin, editors, *The Kirlian Aura*, Anchor Books, New York, 1974.

Leadbeater, C. W., *Man Visible and Invisible*, Theosophical Publishing Society, London, 1920.

Levi, Eliphas, *The History of Magic*, William Rider & Son, London, 1922.

Mesmer, Franz Anton, *De Planetarum Influxu*, Paris, 1766.

Monier-Williams, Monier, *Brahmanism and Hinduism*, Macmillan and Co., New York, 1891.

Montagu, Ashley, *Touching, The Human Significance of Skin*, Harper & Row, New York, 1978.

Moss, Thelma, *The Probability of the Impossible*, J. P. Tarcher, Inc., Los Angeles, 1974.

Murray-Aynsley, Mrs., *Symbolism of the East and the West*, George Redway, London, 1900.

The Mythology of All Races, edited by Canon John Arnott MacCulloch, Marshall Jones Co., Boston, 1932.

Ornstein, Robert E., *The Mind Field*, Grossman Publishers, New York, 1976.

Ostrander, Sheila and Lynn Schroeder, *Psychic Discoveries Behind the Iron Curtain*, Bantam Books, New York, 1970.

Ostrander, Sheila and Lynn Schroeder, *Handbook of Psi Discoveries*, Berkley Publishing Corp., New York, 1974.

Panchadasi, Swami, *The Astral World*, Yoga Publication Society,

Chicago, 1915.

Pancoast, N., *Blue and Red Light*, J. M. Stoddart & Co., Philadelphia, 1877.

Papyrus Ebers, translated from the German by Cyril P. Bryan, Geoffrey Bles, London, 1930.

Park, Willard Z., *Shamanism in Western North America*, Northwestern University, Evanston, Illinois, 1938.

Pleasonton, A. J., *Blue and Sun-Lights*, Claxton, Remsen & Haffelfinger, Philadelphia, 1876.

Pliny, *Natural History*, Henry G. Bohn, London, 1857.

Read, John, *Prelude to Chemistry*, Macmillan, New York, 1937.

Redgrove, H. Stanley, *Alchemy: Ancient and Modern*, William Rider·& Son, Ltd., London, 1922.

Romains, Jules, *Eyeless Sight*, G. P. Putnam's Sons, London, 1924.

Russell, Edward D., *Design for Destiny*, Ballantine Books, New York, 1973.

Singer, Charles, *From Magic to Medicine*, Ernest Benn Ltd., London, 1928.

Solon, Leon V., "Polochromy," *Architectural Record*, New York, 1924.

Spiegelberg, Friedrich, *The Bible of the World*, Viking Press, New York, 1939.

Van der Veer, R. and G. Meijer, *Light and Plant Growth*, Philips Technical Library, Eindhoven, The Netherlands, 1959.

Vernon, M. D., *A Further Study of Visual Perception*, Cambridge University Press, London, 1954.

Vernon, M. D., *The Psychology of Perception*, Penguin Books, Harmondsworth, Middlesex, England, 1966.

Waite, Arthur Edward, *The Book of Ceremonial Magic*, William Rider & Son, London, 1911.

Waite, Arthur Edward, *A New Encyclopedia of Freemasonry*, William Rider & Son, London, 1921.

White, George Starr, *The Story of the Human Aura*, published by the author, Los Angeles, 1928.

Williams, C. A. S., *Outlines of Chinese Symbolism*, Customs College Press, Peiping, China, 1931.

Woolley, C. Leonard, *Ur of the Chaldees*, Charles Scribner's Sons, New York, 1930.

ABOUT THE AUTHOR

Faber Birren is the most widely read authority on color in our time. He is the author of more than two dozen books on the subject and has served as consultant to major businesses and government agencies. Among his most famous works are: *Color: A Survey in Words and Pictures* and *Color Psychology and Color* Therapy, both of which are published by Citadel Press in paperback editions.